THE SEVENTH URBAN FARM FRESH ROMANCE

Dancing at Daybreak

VALERIE COMER

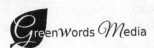

GreenWords Media

Copyright © 2019 Valerie Comer
All rights reserved.
ISBN: 9781988068497

No part of this publication may be reproduced or transmitted for
commercial purposes, except for brief quotations in printed or electronic
reviews, without written permission of the author.

This is a work of fiction set in a redrawn Spokane, Washington.
Businesses and locations are used fictitiously. Any resemblance to actual
persons, living or dead, is coincidental.

The Holy Bible, English Standard Version. ESV® Permanent Text
Edition® (2016). Copyright © 2001 by Crossway Bibles, a publishing
ministry of Good News Publishers. All rights reserved.

The Passion Translation®. Copyright © 2017 by BroadStreet
Publishing® Group, LLC. Used by permission. All rights reserved.
thePassionTranslation.com

The lyrics to *Angels We Have Heard on High* and *It Came upon the Midnight Clear* are found in the public domain.

Cover Art © 2019 Hanna Sandvig, www.bookcoverbakery.com.

First edition, GreenWords Media, 2019

ACKNOWLEDGMENTS

Thank you for being a faithful reader of the Urban Farm Fresh Romance series!

Thanks to Elizabeth Maddrey, first reader and idea-bouncer. Thank you for believing in Dixie and encouraging me to keep going day by day, even when it seemed her restoration would never happen!

Also thank you to beta readers Paula, Karen, Tina, and Joelle. Your comments and prayers and help made a big difference in pulling this story together.

A big thank you to my fabulous editor, Nicole, who sees beyond words, punctuation, and sentence structure to the heart of the story.

I'm also grateful for the Christian Indie Authors Face-book group and my sister bloggers at Inspy Romance. These folks make a difference in my life every single day. I'm thrilled to walk beside them as we tell stories for Jesus!

Thank you to my Facebook friends, followers, street team, and reader group members for prayers, encouragement, and great fellowship.

Thanks to my husband, Jim, for research trips to Spokane and talking through scenarios as needed — to say nothing of everyday love and support — and to my kids and grandgirls for cheering me on and embracing the idiosyncrasies of having an author for a mom and grandmother.

All my love and gratitude goes to Jesus, the One who invited me to experience His unending and passionate love and walks beside me every day. My prayer is that you see His love anew through the pages of this story.

Valerie Comer Bibliography

Urban Farm Fresh Romance

0. Promise of Peppermint (ebook only)
1. Secrets of Sunbeams
2. Butterflies on Breezes
3. Memories of Mist
4. Wishes on Wildflowers
5. Flavors of Forever
6. Raindrops on Radishes
7. Dancing at Daybreak

Saddle Springs Romance

1. The Cowboy's Christmas Reunion
2. The Cowboy's Mixed-Up Matchmaker
3. The Cowboy's Romantic Dreamer
4. The Cowboy's Convenient Marriage

Christmas in Montana Romance

1. More Than a Tiara
2. Other Than a Halo
3. Better Than a Crown

Garden Grown Romance
(Arcadia Valley Romance)

1. Sown in Love (ebook only)
2. Sprouts of Love
3. Rooted in Love
4. Harvest of Love

Farm Fresh Romance

1. Raspberries and Vinegar
2. Wild Mint Tea
3. Sweetened with Honey
4. Dandelions for Dinner
5. Plum Upside Down
6. Berry on Top

Riverbend Romance Novellas

1. Secretly Yours
2. Pinky Promise
3. Sweet Serenade
4. Team Bride
5. Merry Kisses

valeriecomer.com/books

*M*ama, why don't you live here anymore?"

Dixie Wayling set down her fashion magazine and looked over at her five-year-old daughter. Mandy's messy blond hair curtained her face as she bent over a drawing at the table, empty cereal bowls pushed to the side. Dixie listened for the boys for a second but tuned them out when she heard two little voices from the backyard. No screams. All was well.

Mandy pushed her tangles aside and looked at Dixie. "I miss you, Mama."

"Hey, baby, I'm right here."

"But you're not here to tuck me in at night time. Daddy doesn't sing me songs."

"His name is Dan. He's not your daddy." Dixie pulled to her feet. Why did her kid have to talk like this? Oh, she knew. She knew she'd taken the coward's way out... not only once, but a pile of times. She was a poor excuse for humanity. Mom had told her that since she was a kid, and it was true. About the only thing she did well was make more humans... a skill frowned upon by those who thought she should get settled, get married, and get religion, not necessarily in that order.

"God doesn't care about your past," Dan had said earnestly. "He's ready to forgive you and welcome you into His family. He did it for me, and He wants to do it for you. You just have to ask."

So, she'd kicked him out. She'd been getting tired of him, anyway. But then he found out she'd gone off drinking with her girlfriends and forgotten to get a sitter — wasn't Mandy old enough to watch her little brothers? — and returned the favor. He'd moved back in with the kids and told her she could either leave or marry him.

Such romance.

She'd stormed out, but the welcome at Mom's had worn thin after the first couple of weeks. Now she spent most daytimes with the boys while Mandy went to school and Dan to work. Sometimes he dropped them off at a neighborhood daycare instead, but he said her kids needed her more.

She watched them for no pay, like before, only now she had expenses. Of course, she *had* given birth to them. They weren't really Dan's responsibility in any way, except for the youngest. Who knew freewheeling party man Dan Ranta would turn into a grownup when she got pregnant with his kid? He sold used cars back then, and steady jobs were handy for paying rent and buying new clothes. But then his estranged father had a heart attack, and Dan found himself back in the fold, running the family landscaping business.

More money and an actual house — rented, but still — instead of a dinky apartment had been kind of nice at first, until Dan *found Jesus*. Dixie bit back a snort.

Chewing on the end of a pencil crayon, Mandy watched her mama from deep brown eyes. "Daddy says he wants to have a wedding, and we can be a real family like everybody else."

Dixie crossed the space, kicking one of Henry's shoes into a pile of plastic blocks. She glanced out the patio door in time to see Buddy give the toddler a shove and send him to his diapered rear in the yellowing grass. No screaming. Whew. Dan had done a good thing getting them this house. The yard was kid-proof with not even a gate, so they could let the kids in and out without any worry. Dixie wasn't *that* bad a mother. She wouldn't let them loose in the wild without supervision.

She turned back to Mandy and tried to force her fingers through the tangles. "Run get a brush. You look a mess."

"Okay, Mama." Mandy slid off the chair and darted up the stairs.

Dixie picked up the drawing her daughter had been working on. It seemed to contain a humanoid shape, legs and arms outstretched, wearing a... tutu?

Something stabbed deep inside her, not for the first time. She was missing so much of her kids' younger years. Mandy had been in kindergarten for a couple of months already, and Dixie hadn't even met her teacher. Dan dropped Mandy off at Bridgeview Elementary on his way to work and arranged for an older neighbor kid to walk her home every afternoon in case Henry was napping.

Dan was so considerate. He really was a nice guy. He might even pay for dance lessons for Mandy if Dixie asked. He'd been such a pushover, until he asked Dixie to marry him, and she said no. Because of the Jesus thing. Dan had only gotten guilty about them living together. She'd also said no because her mom's words rang in her ear, that she didn't need no man. It was Mom's favorite litany. Men were weak. Men were dumb. Men were needed for only one thing, and wasn't the planet full enough with over seven billion inhabitants? Then she'd look at Dixie's three kids and shake her head, her lips pursed in disapproval.

Yeah, pleasing Mom was impossible anyway. Pleasing Jesus would be no easier. Dixie might not be the sharpest crayon in the box, but she knew she wasn't good enough for God, no matter what Dan said about repentance and forgiveness and all that. He'd never been as bad as her. There were limits to what God could excuse.

I mean, look at me and my mess.

Mandy clattered down the stairs, neon pink hairbrush in hand. "Here, Mama. Don't pull too hard. It hurts my head." She slid onto the chair, her back to Dixie.

Dan had threatened to chop off Mandy's hair to make it easier to care for, but he was a pushover for the little girl's tears and had relented. Then he'd seen a YouTube video where some guy vacuumed his daughter's hair into a ponytail, and now he was all pro. But today was Saturday, and he'd left the house with the kids still in their pajamas.

Dixie didn't mind doing Mandy's hair once a week. She tugged the brush through the lower snarls and worked her way up to the scalp. Then she fingered the long strands into sections.

Mandy's hands covered hers. "What are you doing, Mama?"

"Thought I'd give you a French braid. Would you like that?"

"Oh! Can you? Tieri's mommy makes her hair into a crown for dance. It's so pretty."

Her daughter was five-and-a-half and Dixie hadn't braided her hair in so long Mandy couldn't remember? Failure two thousand three hundred eighty-five as a mother. Not that she was keeping count.

DAN RANTA PULLED his landscaping truck into the drive beside Dixie's older car. She was still here. Good. Ever since that time in July when the neighbor called him because Dixie had left the kids alone, he worried all day, every day. A guy could only do so much. He had a business to run. He needed the work to keep a roof over their heads and some stability for those young lives. He might not be Mandy or Buddy's biological father, but they were his responsibility now, and he wasn't the shirking kind.

If only...

Dan shook his head, shoved the truck door open, grabbed his backpack and lunchbox, and headed for the house. He eased the door open, braced against what he might find.

No one was yelling or crying. Mandy's giggle mingled with Dixie's. He hadn't heard that in a long, long time. A breath slid out. *Thank You, Jesus.*

He tried not to take moments of harmony for granted.

Tried not to segment each day in columns with bad, okay, and good as headers. He set his things inside the door and toed off his grass-stained steel-toed boots.

"Daddy's home!" Buddy charged down the short hallway and flung himself at Dan's knees.

Dan stiffened for impact as well as for Dixie's voice reminding the boy that he wasn't his daddy. For once, she skipped the opportunity. "Hey, Buddy!" He swung the almost-four-year-old into his arms and gave him a whisker rub. "Been good for your mama today?"

"Buddy always good."

Not to hear Dixie tell it... or from Dan's own experience. He chuckled. "Good job. What did you do?"

"Me'n Henry play tag."

Dan cringed. Didn't that just sound like a way for the bigger boy to chase and hit the smaller one? But the toddler wasn't crying. At least, not right now. Dan tucked a squealing Buddy under his arm like a football as he entered the living room beyond the staircase.

Dixie and Mandy looked up from the book they were reading on the sofa, and Mandy jumped up and ran over.

He hugged her against his leg, noting the braided crown, as he set Buddy down. Henry toddled over and Dan gave the little guy a quick hug as well. But his gaze stayed riveted on the children's mother.

Dixie looked happier today than sometimes, and he couldn't help smiling back. Her blond hair brushed the front of her top. He loved that one on her. Had he ever told her? But this might not be the moment, since the white lace reminded him of a wedding dress, and she shot that dream down in a big fat hurry every time he brought it up.

Dixie bit her lip as she took in the little ones crowding around him. Her eyebrows peaked as her gaze collided with his for an instant. "Hey, Dan." She surged off the couch and grabbed her big red purse. "I thought you'd never get here. See you Monday."

"Stay for dinner? I brought pizza. It's in the truck."

She smoothed the lacy top over her narrow hips with her free hand. "No, that's okay. I'm going out with some friends."

"Stay, Mama!" Mandy dashed over to her mother and clung to her arm. "Maybe we can watch a movie. Please?"

Dixie patted the little girl's back. "Not this time, baby. I have to go."

"I'll walk you out." Dan held the toddler to Mandy, who slung the little guy to her nonexistent hip.

"Not necessary."

"I know, but I have to grab the pizza, anyway."

Dixie skirted around him as she tugged on her sweater. "Suit yourself."

He hurried after her and opened the door as he shoved his feet into worn sneakers. "Dixie, wait."

But she didn't. He caught up to her beside the gray Mazda. "How's it running?"

She rolled her eyes. "Fine, Dan. It's not your responsibility."

"Sure, it is. I bought it for you."

"You want it back? Is that what this is all about?"

Dan let out a sharp breath. "No, of course not. It's yours, no matter what. I only care about you." He longed to sweep his fingers over her cheek, feel the petal-soft skin one more time. "Looks like you and the kids had a good day?"

"It was okay."

"Mandy's hair looks pretty."

Dixie shrugged, still not meeting his gaze. "Yeah. It made her happy."

"Thanks." Dan jammed his hands into his jeans pockets. In the old days when she got pouty like this, he'd have just kissed her until she smiled. Or maybe taken her off to bed. But he'd had a come-to-Jesus experience last spring, and he was determined to treat her with respect, whether she made it easy or not.

She wasn't making it easy.

Not sashaying in those skinny jeans and snug top. Not when she alternated between playing hard-to-get and throwing herself at him. Today was ice. He never knew ahead of time. The only things she was consistent about these days were jabbing at his newfound faith every chance she got... and refusing to marry him.

He took a breath. "I wanted to talk to you about Buddy's birthday. It's in just a couple of weeks. November eighth, right?"

"Yeah." She reached for the door handle.

Dan stayed in her way, and she pulled her hand back. "What do you want to do for a party?"

Dixie stared up at him. "He's just a little kid. He doesn't need a fuss."

"Fran Amato's little boy, Luca, turned four in August, and she had a party for him."

He could see the battle on Dixie's face. Even she hadn't been able to come up with any evidence to support her earlier theory that Fran was his other girlfriend. Fran was a nice, married woman from Bridgeview Bible Church who ran a private daycare in her home a few blocks away. She was Dan's backup plan for the boys on days Dixie didn't show before he had to leave for work... which averaged once a week.

"How nice for them."

That was all Dixie could come up with? He pushed ahead. "I don't really want to do a party with a bunch of little kids, but how about a family time on a Sunday afternoon? We could get pizza or burgers and go to a playground or the children's museum, maybe?"

He hated the need that came through in his voice. He hated putting himself at Dixie's mercy. He hated that he had to beg her to spend time with not just her kids, but him.

She stepped closer and rested her hands on his chest, sweat-stained T-shirt and all. "Maybe."

Dan stilled, forcing his hands to stay deep in his pockets as he inhaled the sweet fragrance of her. It took a minute before he could trust his voice. "What kind of maybe?"

"Quit with the Jesus talk, and we can go back to how things were before." Her long fingernails walked across his chest, each leaving a pinpoint of pain. "We were good together."

He took a big step backward and smacked into her car. "Don't use me as a pawn against the kids, Dix. They don't deserve it. They deserve a mom who's part of their life. Marry—"

"No." Dixie leaned into his face. "That's not how this game works, Daniel Ranta. You want to win? You've got the magic card in *your* hand. Play it." She pivoted on her heel, jerked the car door open, and climbed inside.

Without a backward glance, she drove away, taking Dan's heart with her.

2

I'm here to pick up the boys." Dixie stood in Fran Amato's doorway. "I was only five minutes late. Dan should have waited for me."

"Come on in, Dixie." Fran held the door open with a smile. "Dan probably didn't want Mandy late for school. Would you like a coffee?"

Late schmate. It was kindergarten, for crying out loud. "No, thank you. Just the boys."

"That's too bad. Luca and Buddy dove right into building a fort out of blankets in his bedroom. They'll be so disappointed."

Dixie pulled herself to her full height, all five-foot-three. "But—"

"Aw, come in for a bit. It seems I hardly know you at all, and that's a shame since we're practically neighbors."

Against her will, Dixie took a step inside, then another, until the other woman closed the door against the fall drizzle. Being almost neighbors was a joke, though. Dixie didn't really live in Bridgeview, not since Dan kicked her out, but

Mom's apartment wasn't that many blocks out of the river-front Spokane neighborhood. "Well, I, um..."

"Mamamama!" Henry toddled over and patted Dixie's leg.

"Coffee or tea?" Fran asked from the nearby kitchen, a half-full coffeepot in hand.

Coffee was for hangovers, though Dan mainlined the stuff all the time. "Herbal tea, if you have it."

The other woman laughed as she reached to fill a turquoise kettle. "Do you know my cousin Jasmine? If you do, you'll understand why I have about eight kinds of locally foraged herbs in my cupboard right now. Let's see, nettle, chamomile—"

"Chamomile, please." Whatever nettle was. Dixie didn't want to know.

Fran poured a coffee and dribbled some cream in it while the kettle heated.

Dixie sat at the kitchen table and lifted Henry to her lap. He slapped at the table and grinned up at her. Her heart caught at how much he looked like his daddy. Why couldn't things be simpler with Dan? Why had she finally latched onto a decent guy only to lose him to religion?

The doorbell rang, but Fran didn't take two steps toward it before the door popped open and a young woman about Dixie's age entered carrying a toddler.

Henry squirmed to get down. "Baba."

"Hey, Henry. Yes, I brought the baby. Not that Gavin is so much younger than you are." The woman plopped the small boy on the floor then flipped back her long dark hair as she looked at Dixie. "I'm Ava, by the way. You must be Henry's mom."

"Yes. Dixie Wayling. Nice to meet you." It seemed like Fran's daycare was a happening place. The few times Dixie had been by before, she'd turned down the invitation. Probably a good idea to see where her sons spent so much time, though.

The kettle whistled. "Time for coffee or tea, Ava?" asked Fran. "Or do you have classes today?"

Ava grimaced. "Today and every day. Dafne will be here to pick up Gavin after three."

"Sounds good. One of these days you need to come by when you have more than five seconds. Seems like ages since we've caught up."

"I know. I'll try. Promise." She patted the little guy on the head. "Bye, Gav. Nice to meet you, Dixie. Have a good day, Fran." Fluttering her fingers, she dashed out the door.

"Always so busy with classes." Fran poured boiling water over herbs, and the rich aroma of chamomile permeated the space. "Did you go to college, Dixie?"

"No. I wasn't much for school." She'd made it through high school by the skin of her teeth, and that was enough. Just lately she'd begun to regret not having any goals for her life, though. Not quite twenty-five with three kids. Ugh.

"Having a family childcare home wasn't what I always wanted, either." Fran's eyes grew large. "Not that I don't enjoy having your boys and little Gavin and a few other drop-ins. I do have a degree in early childhood, but I wanted to stay home with Tieri and Luca, and we couldn't quite afford it on Tad's income with the city. Tad's my husband."

Of course, Fran was married. Dixie and Dan's old apartment complex was full of fluid families with partners coming and going. She and Dan had practically been the longest standing couple in the place by the time they left. Moving to a rental house in an established neighborhood had only reminded Dixie that some people lived a different normal.

She accepted the cup of tea and the jar filled with honey, even as the urge to grab the boys and run swelled over her. But she still hadn't seen Buddy, and Henry had just offered a stuffed giraffe to Gavin then snatched it away while the other boy stared, thumb in mouth. Besides, she really was kind of starving for female companionship. Days home alone with the kids dragged on. "Thanks."

Fran set a plate of cookies on the table then bent and offered one to each of the toddlers before taking a seat at the table. She smiled at Dixie. "Tell me all about yourself."

Um, no. That wasn't happening.

"Did you grow up in Spokane?"

"Yeah, but not in as nice a neighborhood as this." Her kids really were lucky to have Dan in their lives. Too bad she couldn't say the same for herself.

"Siblings?" Fran took a sip.

Dixie shook her head. "Nope, just me and my mom." And a revolving door of men.

"I've got one younger brother. Rob lives in Montana with his wife and three kids." Fran glanced at Dixie. "His wife had two already when they met. She'd had a rough upbringing and all, but she and Rob are so happy together now. They had a baby boy last Christmas."

"How nice for them." Whatever *rough upbringing* meant. Could it match Dixie's mess? Not likely. Some days it felt like she'd cornered the market.

Fran's warm smile probed the crust of Dixie's shell. "It really is. I know Bren had a hard time believing in her worth. In Rob's love for her." She chuckled. "In God's love, too."

And here came the God-talk that seemed so prevalent in Bridgeview. Great. "God's never done anything for me."

"Oh, but He has. He created you. He loves you. He offers hope for the future filled with His joy."

Dixie shook her head and rolled her eyes. "Now you sound like Dan, but I'm here to tell you God doesn't *give* joy. He kills it."

Fran reached out a hand but stopped just before covering Dixie's. "Oh, no, honey. I'm so sorry you feel that way. If you turn toward Him instead of away, you'll find the opposite is true. He'll welcome you and shower you with peace and comfort."

"That's great for you." Dixie surged to her feet. "I really need to be going now. Where did you say Buddy is?" She plucked Henry off the floor and swung him to her hip.

"Aw, I wasn't trying to push you. I just get so excited about Jesus. Please stay and finish your tea. I promise to tone it down."

No way. Dixie was out of here.

꩜

HENRY ON HIS HIP, Dan watched as Dixie peeled out of the driveway, tires spinning in the gravel. Not only had she been late this morning — meaning she'd had to pick the boys up from Fran's — but she wouldn't even meet his gaze when he got home. He'd walked in, and she'd jumped off the sofa, grabbed her purse, and all but jogged for the door. No flirting. No accusations. No nothing.

He heaved a deep sigh. What was going on with her? And was it ever going to end? He'd been so hopeful a few months ago.

"Hey, neighbor."

Dan swung toward the house next door, where Jacob Riehl came through the side gate, locking a bleating goat in the backyard. "Hey."

"Don't see you around much. How are things going?"

"Could be better." No doubt his neighbor had heard Dixie's dramatic exit. "But I'm keeping busy, wrapping up the season. You?"

Jacob shoved his hands into trouser pockets. "Yeah, and I'm leaving for Africa for two weeks on Friday. Sure wish I could take Eden on one of these trips."

"You work for a solar company, don't you?"

"Yep. Global Sunbeams. We do a lot of charity work in Mozambique, Malawi, and other countries in that part of eastern Africa. Cyclones destroyed some of our installations, so a team of us are headed over for repairs."

"That's cool." Dan grimaced. "You're doing something that really makes a difference, and I'm mowing rich peoples' yards. Something anyone could do."

"Don't knock it, Ranta. We all have our own part to play, you know? A guy with three little kids to take care of can't be off jaunting around the world for weeks at a time. They need you."

It probably wasn't the time to ask if Jacob and his wife were planning to start a family. Not while Dan had done everything backward, a point even his anti-Christian father hammered home every chance he got.

Jacob leaned closer, his mouth twisted into a half-smile. "Mind you, Eden's not happy my work takes me away so often. She gets it, but still."

"Dixie wouldn't put up with it, that's for sure." Dan shook his head. "Not that she puts up with *me*, exactly, anyway." Good thing his son was too young to understand the conversation.

"She sounded a little upset when she left."

"She was." Dan eyed his neighbor. They must be close in age. Just look what a difference an education, a long-standing faith, and a wealthy family could make — not that Jacob and Eden lived like they had money. Eden worked for the city in animal control, a job Dan wouldn't want for anything.

"Some of the guys from church just started getting together Wednesday mornings to pray with one another. Interested in joining us?"

Dan shook his head. "Full slate on Wednesdays." And every day. Work would be spottier over the winter, depending on how much it snowed.

Jacob grinned. "It's at six in the morning."

"Doesn't much help since I have to be here with the kids until Dixie arrives." Or until she didn't, as the case might be. Half her problem tonight was that he'd taken the boys to Fran's this morning, but how was he supposed to know she was on her way if she didn't call? Kindergarten for Mandy started at eight-fifteen and Dan's first client expected him at eight-thirty clear over in Greenwood. Dixie knew he couldn't sit around waiting for her to show up whenever she got around to it. He had a business to run.

"Eden and I talked about that. She offered to pop over here for that hour. Some of the guys have to start work at seven-thirty or eight, so we're punctual about ending at seven. Eden doesn't start until nine, so she'd still have plenty of time to get ready for work if she was here with the kids."

Dan stared at his neighbor and shifted Henry to his other hip. "Seriously? She doesn't even really know us. That's thoughtful and all, but I can't ask for charity."

"You're not asking. She's offering. She's tried to get to know Dixie a little but hasn't gotten very far."

Dan heaved a sigh. "Dixie is... wary. To her way of thinking, everyone in the neighborhood judges her and talks about her behind her back."

"I'm sorry she feels that way, man. I think Eden's not the only woman who's tried to extend some friendship. We all just want to surround your family with love and support." Jacob grinned. "And I think the men's prayer breakfast would help you see that."

Something eased inside Dan. "You didn't say anything about breakfast before. That changes everything."

"We meet at Bridgeview Bakery and Bistro. Hailey opens up an hour early for us on Wednesdays. It won't be full service since the staff has their usual prep to do, but she'll offer coffee and a set breakfast each week for a good price. I usually walk over. It's just a few blocks."

"Are you sure Eden wouldn't mind?"

"Positive. It was her idea. She asked me to mention it to you if I saw you."

"You know what? Let's give it a try. But you're off to Africa."

Jacob shrugged. "Not until Friday, so we can go together this week. Besides, you know everyone. You went to school with half of them, didn't you?"

"Yeah, I guess I did. The Santoro guys and Nathan Hamelin, anyway."

"Like I said, half." The other man grinned. "Just want you to know that we're all here for you. We already pray for both you and Dixie. I'm confident God will answer our prayers on your behalf." He chucked Henry under the chin. "This little guy will grow up in a Christian home with two parents."

Henry chortled.

"Wish I was as sure as you." Dan mussed his son's hair. "But it seems farther away than ever before."

3

*T*oo bad they weren't a real family. At times like this, it would be far too easy for Dixie to let her guard down and pretend, or even go along with Dan's preposterous offers of marriage and permanence.

If only permanence were a thing, but it wasn't. Look at Mom, after all. And, while Dan's parents had stuck together, Dixie would never put up with Dave Senior the way Yvonne did. Talk about domineering. Even his heart attack and semi-retirement two years before had done little to soothe his bluster.

Dixie shuddered.

"Cold?" Dan leaned closer where he sat at the picnic table, the brush of his arm sparking off her shoulder. "I've got a spare jacket in the trunk."

She blinked the scene back into focus. Fran and Tad Amato sat across from them, Tad laughing at something Fran said, his eyes soft as he looked at her. The four older kids — Tieri, Mandy, Buddy, and Luca — ran and climbed and swung on the nearby play structure while Henry dug in the sand with a stick he'd found.

"No, I'm good." She shifted slightly away from Dan so he wouldn't get any ideas. This was only for Buddy's birthday, after all. Dan shouldn't harbor thoughts they were going to hang out on a regular basis. Even when they'd lived together, they'd never done family-type stuff with others. It'd mostly been parties when the kids were asleep.

Buddy whooshed down the slide and collided with Henry, sending the toddler sprawled in the sand, screaming.

Before Dixie could get to her feet, Dan was halfway there. He squatted and gave Buddy what-for even while scooping Henry against his shoulder. Henry's pudgy hands cradled Dan's neck. Then Buddy patted Henry's back and wrapped his arms around Dan, too.

Man, he was so good with the kids. Her heart squeezed. He didn't seem to remember that Mandy and Buddy weren't even his.

"Do you have any drama experience?"

Dixie blinked at Fran. Where had that question come from? Did the other woman think Dixie was some kind of diva?

Fran laughed. "Music? Dance? Anything?"

"I... what are you getting at?" Because Dixie hadn't been born yesterday. Divulging too much too soon could get her locked into something she wanted no part of.

"The church puts on a Christmas program every year. Somehow, I'm in charge of it, and it's really not my area of expertise. That and it takes more than one person to pull it together."

Dixie shook her head. "I don't do church."

"I know, but you're good with the kids, and if you have any experience...?"

Not experience that counted. "I don't think so."

"The girls have already been practicing their choreography for it." Fran glanced toward the play structure. "Mandy is a natural."

Dan slid back onto the bench, still holding Henry. "Mandy wanted dance lessons, but she told us too late. Classes were already full, so she's on the cancelation list for January." He nudged Dixie. "Dixie's got great moves."

Heat swarmed up her face. What would his churchy friends think of that comment?

"We're practicing in the church basement Tuesdays after school. You could bring the boys. Luca will be with me — there's a playroom right off the meeting room."

A church basement was still church, right?

"Kass is in charge most years," Fran went on. "Have you met her? She and her cousin own Bridgeview Bakery and Bistro. But Kass and Wesley got married in September and, believe it or not, she's puking pregnant already."

"We haven't really met." Dan had gone to the wedding, and Dixie had watched the kids. Weddings were not for her, especially when she didn't know the couple and didn't want to know them. Weddings gave Dan ideas. He'd been to a few in the past couple of years. She'd seen the aftermath.

"Adriana is usually big into the planning, too. Her and Rebekah. But they both have newborns. Bridgeview is having a baby boom, and that's great. But it's sure hard to find dependable volunteers these days."

No one had called Dixie dependable since ever. And Fran knew better, too, what with all the times Dixie flaked out and Dan dropped the boys off at daycare. Yet, Fran was still asking. She was right about one thing. Dixie was bored stiff. Would a regular outing with the kids be so bad?

Church. It was a church thing. That's what would be so bad. She shook her head. "I don't think so."

"Aw, I was hoping you'd give it some thought."

Dan's arm pressed against Dixie's on the picnic table. "You know what might work, Fran? Dixie probably wouldn't mind if you dropped Luca off at the house when you go over to the church. Then you wouldn't have to worry about him interrupting you and stuff."

The other woman's face lit up. "That would be a help, for sure. I mean, an assistant would be better, but the boys do play so well together."

Dixie knew when she was cornered. "Sure. That'd be fine."

"That's settled, then. Ava might be able to juggle her schedule and help with the choreography. She's taking dance, you know."

No, Dixie didn't know. "But she has a baby, too."

"Gavin? He's her nephew."

Dixie blinked. She'd seen Ava a few times dropping the little guy off at Fran's over the past few weeks.

"Gavin is her sister Dafne's boy. Daf got pregnant in her Junior year of high school, and her family is helping her raise him. My aunt cut back her hours at work..."

Fran prattled on, but Dixie tuned her out. A member of the exalted Santoro clan had a baby even younger than Dixie'd been at Mandy's conception? Although, she knew the family wasn't completely comprised of paragons. She'd hung out with Fran's cousin Basil, after all. It had been after

Henry's birth, and she'd been so tired of being a mother and of Dan's constant hovering, she'd made a play for Basil. She'd pretty much caught him, too, but then he'd tried to run a police checkpoint with her in the car and gotten nailed with a DUI. After a month in jail, he'd left Spokane. Dan had probably threatened him. Dan's jealousy and anger had been something to behold.

And yet, somehow, she was still with him. Sort of with him. He refused to stay out of her life on account of Henry, unlike the older kids' dads. Both Brandon and Scott had vanished into thin air at the first sign of puke, let alone diapers. Good riddance.

She wanted Dan to stay. Wanted him to be the good guy in her sordid life. Without religion, he'd been a giant step up from previous boyfriends. Now he was so solid it hurt. She couldn't deal, and she couldn't get rid of him.

DAN HOISTED Henry to his shoulders as Buddy and Mandy ran ahead to the car. Dixie'd been kind of quiet today, but at least she'd come and been somewhat civil to the Amatos. He snagged her hand and, for once, she didn't pull away. "Thanks," he said.

"For?" Her eyebrows arched as she looked up at him.

"For making Buddy's birthday fun." She shrugged and tried to pull away, but he held tighter. "He's happy today."

"Well, yeah. You spoil him."

He chuckled. "It's not spoiling to go to the park with takeout burgers and a grocery store birthday cake."

"You got him a gift."

He'd given the store-wrapped box to the little boy before they'd left for the park, because who wanted to pack extra stuff around? Buddy'd been excited about the toy cars and racetrack set and whined about leaving it home for a few hours. No wonder he and his sister were standing at the car, waiting for the rest of the family. Not that they were one.

Dan squeezed Dixie's fingers. "Of course. It's his birthday."

This time he let her pull away, and she shoved her hands in her jeans pockets. "You're not even his father."

Back to that tired old argument? "He's my son's brother, and that's close enough for me."

She rolled her eyes and popped the locks on the car. Buddy scrambled in, and Dan swung Henry into his seat in the middle and clipped his harness. By the time Dan backed out to allow Mandy access, Dixie had settled into the driver's seat. Well, it *was* her car, but she'd let him drive on the way to the park. Now she was proving she was still the boss of herself.

Like he'd been under any illusions.

Dan slid into the passenger seat without commenting. It wouldn't do any good, anyway.

Dad's words rampaged through Dan's head. Dad never lost an opportunity to remind him what a loser Dixie was and how stupid Dan was to be taking care of her kids. Enabling her, Dad called it. Imagine what would happen if Dan told his parents he actually loved Dixie. The explosion would blast the roof right off their house.

But the question was, *did* he love her? And if he did, why? Yeah, he'd thought they had a good thing going. That she'd only been promiscuous because she hadn't met the right guy yet. Obviously, he was that guy. He'd tame her wild ways and they'd get married and live happily ever after.

Even after he'd put his trust in Jesus a few months ago, he'd thought it would only be a matter of time, but his father was right. Dan was stupid. Dixie was never going to come around.

"Daddy, can I—"

"He's not your daddy!" Dixie exploded from the driver's seat. The car even swerved a little at her vehemence.

"Da-Danny, can I play cars at home?"

"Of course, you can, Buddy. That racing set belongs to you. You can play it anytime."

"No, he can't." Dixie shot Dan a glare.

He raised his eyebrows in her direction.

"I went along with your thing in the park, but now I'm taking the kids to my mom's. She's his grandmother, you know, and it's only fair she gets to see him on his birthday."

No point reminding Dixie the boy's birthday had been Friday, and she'd had him all day while Dan was at work. No point reminding her that Eunice didn't have a grandmotherly bone in her body. He couldn't use reason when she got like this.

"But I want to play cars, Mama!"

"Later, Buddy. We're going to drop Dan off at the house."

A few minutes later, he stood in his driveway and waved to the kids with a smile. It wouldn't do for them to sense his fear that he might never see them again.

"Hey, Dan."

He glanced over to see Jacob raking leaves in the front

yard next door. "Hi, Jacob. I didn't know you were back from Africa."

"Got back yesterday, and I'm trying to get my body back in this time zone as well as autumn instead of spring. Tricky stuff."

Sounded believable. Dan hadn't ever been anywhere to know for sure. Well, Montana, but one time zone barely counted.

"You been going to the prayer breakfast while I was away?"

Dan nodded. "Yeah. Weird, though. I don't really fit in."

"Oh? How's that?"

"Most of the guys are married."

Jacob studied him. "Some aren't. Alex. Peter."

"Peter's going to pop the question to Sadie any day now."

"True... but why does it matter?"

Dan took off his baseball cap and shoved his hand through his hair. Haircut time again. "It just does. We don't have much in common. My life is... complicated."

"Everybody's got something."

"Which one of those men has anything half as weird going on as I do?"

Jacob grinned. "You've got a doozie, that's for sure. But it seems to me like you've chosen to stay in it."

"Not following."

"Like you said, you're *not* married to her. You haven't made any vows, and her kids aren't your responsibility, other than the little guy. Wouldn't it be easier—?"

"Are you saying I should just walk away?" Dan narrowed his eyes. "That doesn't sound like you."

"Have you considered that you're enabling her to keep living this way?"

"Now you sound like my dad."

"He's got to be right some of the time." Jacob leaned on the rake. "I know it sounds harsh, but maybe what she needs is to be cut loose."

"I'm not going to lie and say this is easy. It's not. But isn't sticking around the right thing to do? She's the mother of my son. I have to make it work somehow." How could he show his face around the community, around the church, if he pushed Dixie away? Who would look after the kids? Wait. She'd take them. He wouldn't have to find a sitter. He'd be free like a single guy, like he'd been when he met Dixie three years ago. She already had Mandy and Buddy when he moved in with her.

A new fear shot ice through his veins. What if she got pregnant again, with some other man's baby? She might do it just to spite Dan, like she'd been seeing Basil Santoro after Henry's birth.

"I can't lose her, Jacob. I can't." But could he keep going like this?

"There's a story in the Bible that comes to mind. Been digging in the Old Testament much?"

"Not a lot. My sister told me to read the gospels, and Pastor Tomas has been preaching out of Paul's books lately."

"Okay, you know that the Jews were God's chosen people, right? He made a covenant with them, but they kept wandering off to worship the gods of the nations around them. They just couldn't seem to stick with the love of the One who'd set them apart."

Like Dixie couldn't seem to be satisfied with Dan's love. She was only angry that he wouldn't sleep with her anymore.

"During that time of history, God called a slew of prophets to preach to the people and tell them what they were doing was wrong and that they should repent and turn back to God. There's a bunch of books between Psalms and the New Testament called the prophets. There's some heavy going in those books — I'm not going to lie — but they show how much God tried to get their attention and love."

Dan didn't want to put himself up there with God, but he kind of got it.

"Hosea was one of those prophets. God told him to marry a prostitute named Gomer. Problem was, she wasn't faithful to Hosea. She kept sleeping with other men, but God told Hosea to keep taking her back."

"Uh huh." He wasn't sure he liked where this was going. How close to home it struck.

"God didn't tell Hosea to do that because it was the smartest or even the best thing to do. He was making a point, demonstrating for all Israel to see how the situation was with God and His people. That even when they kept worshiping other deities, God still loved them and didn't break His part of the covenant."

"That all seems to indicate I'm doing the right thing by sticking with Dixie." If so, why wasn't his heart lighter?

"There are some differences. That was an object lesson for a particular time in history. To say nothing of the fact that God and the nation of Israel had made vows to one another."

Yeah, and Dan and Dixie hadn't. He hadn't given much thought to a wedding before he'd found faith in Jesus. In today's society, especially in their circle of friends, no one cared.

"Here's the thing, Dan. Marriage is sacred. It really is. It's not something anyone should do lightly. What good would it do those kids if you married their mother and then you got divorced a year or so down the road?"

Dan took a step back. "I'm not sure you realize what you're saying here."

The sympathy on the other man's face belied those words. "Have you prayed about it? I know you're praying for Dixie's salvation. We all are. But what if she never comes to faith in Jesus? What if it's not God's will for you to marry her? What then?"

"How could it not be?"

Jacob shook his head. "I can't answer that. All I know is, Dixie's salvation and your relationship with her are two separate things. One does not automatically lead to the other."

"That doesn't even make sense, man."

"Two wrongs don't make a right, Dan. They really don't."

i!" Fran stood at the door, eyebrows raised. "I was expecting Dan."

Of course, she was. Dixie beckoned the woman in. "He had to work late. I'll call Luca. The boys are upstairs."

Mandy bounded in from Fran's car. "Mama, it is so fun!" She squeezed her arms around Dixie's middle. "Tieri and me and some other kids are angels."

Dixie's eyebrows shot up. "Dancing angels?"

Fran laughed as she shut the door behind her, closing out the brisk November air. "School-age angels are busy little creatures who are certainly not into sitting on fluffy clouds playing harps."

"What's a harp?" Mandy wanted to know.

"It's..." Fran paused. "A musical instrument with strings."

"Oh, a guitar." The little girl nodded wisely.

"Not exactly. I'll show you a picture sometime." Fran rubbed Mandy's shoulder then turned back to Dixie. "So, yes, dancing angels. Dancing for the whole cast, actually, because why not?"

"I thought the church thinks dancing is a terrible sin." Only one of eighteen thousand reasons to avoid Christianity.

Her friend chuckled, crinkle lines around her eyes proving laughter was a big part of her life. "At its core, dancing is moving one's body to music. Some ways of dancing can lead to impure thoughts and actions, but it sure doesn't have to. It can be a graceful expression of how much we love God, too. It can be a form of worship."

"Huh." Could that be true? Worship didn't sound nearly as much fun as dancing with a hot guy. Dan used to — Dixie blocked that train of thought. He was such a killjoy now, which somehow made him more attractive than ever. Who'd have guessed she'd be drawn to maturity and self-restraint? There was, apparently, a first for everything.

Dixie turned to the staircase. "Luca! Your mom's here." She looked at Fran. "Is Tieri waiting in the car? Sorry I didn't have Luca ready. I wasn't sure what time you'd be here."

"She'll be fine for a sec. Dan's a few minutes late, and I'm a few minutes early, I guess."

"I'm so glad you're here, Mama." Mandy clung to Dixie's arm. "I like dance at church on Tuesday, but I miss seeing you."

Dixie pulled the little girl closer. "I miss you, too." Strangely, it was true. While Luca played well with Buddy and Henry, the last couple of Tuesdays had been strange without Mandy bounding in after school.

"Stay, Mama," whispered Mandy.

"I can't, baby."

Fran offered a sympathetic smile as the four-year-olds scooted down the carpeted stairs on their backsides, giggling the whole way. "You should come by and watch the practice next week. Just let me know not to drop Luca off. There's the playroom at the church with lots for them to do. Henry, too."

"I'll see." Curiosity about dancing angels might lure her in, just once. "When's the big show?"

"The last Sunday before Christmas. The program starts at seven and there are treats and hot cocoa downstairs afterward. Everyone in Bridgeview comes. I know you'll love it."

Right. As though Fran knew anything about Dixie. "Maybe." It was still a month away. Anything could happen. Anything besides Dixie falling for all this Jesus stuff, although it was sometimes tempting to pretend just to get Dan off her back. But then he'd want to marry her, and there was just no way that could end well. No, Dixie was good at faking it for a good cause, but no one could sustain that kind of pretense indefinitely.

"Into your jacket, Luca. Time to go. Daddy's got supper ready."

A normal family where parents tag-teamed to take care of things. Dan wanted that. Why couldn't she just relent and give it to him? Would marrying him be so bad?

Luca dragged his feet as he came toward his mom, who held his jacket out for him. "I want to play with Buddy longer. Why doesn't he ever come play at our house anymore?"

Dixie gave a nervous laugh. All because she was doing her best to turn over a new leaf and be a responsible adult, which meant arriving to watch the boys before Dan left with Mandy.

"Come for coffee one day soon!" Fran urged. "As friends."

"Maybe." It was true the boys had fun together. It was true Dixie went crazy being house-bound. But Fran was so much older than her and so... churchy.

"Hope you do. Drop in anytime." Fran opened the door and nudged Luca toward it. "Thanks for coming, Mandy. You're doing a great job."

Mandy beamed.

Beyond Fran, Dan's truck pulled up to the curb. Of course, Dixie's and Fran's cars blocked the driveway. He wouldn't whine about it, though. He'd just move his truck later. Dixie watched him swing out of the cab, gather his lunchbox and thermos, and stride across the street.

He was so tall and lean and, well, hot even in jeans and his dark green Ranta Landscaping hoodie and a ball cap that covered most of his slightly unruly dark blond hair. Every time she saw him, no matter how hard she tried to tune him out, her blood hummed. They'd been so good together before this religious kick.

Dan opened Fran's car door for her and mussed Luca's hair while he chatted with Fran. But when he closed the car door and met Dixie's gaze, his entire face altered. Softened. She could see his love even from twenty feet away.

No.

Religion was a party-pooper, remember? She wasn't going to play Dan's game. She'd made her own set of rules for her life and, if he wanted to be part of it, he'd follow them. She could out-wait him.

Only, could she? It had been nearly six months already, and he showed no signs of giving up religion.

Fran tapped her horn as she backed out onto the street then drove away. And Dan stood in front of Dixie, his blue eyes warmed by the grin on his face. "Hey, how was your day?"

Dixie pushed away from the door jamb she'd been leaning on. "Okay. I'll grab my stuff and be out of your hair."

Dan looked past her, but none of the kids charged at him for once. "Got a question for you."

She stiffened and wrapped her arms around her middle. "Oh?"

"Would you come to my parents' house with me for Thanksgiving dinner on Thursday? Linnea and Logan will be in town."

Dixie rolled her eyes. "Your parents hate me."

Dan shook his head. "Maybe Dad, but he hates everyone except my brother. Mom asked me to invite you."

"I find that hard to believe."

His grin widened. "Not lying." He reached for her arm, but his hand dropped away before he touched her.

What would happen if she just took one step forward and wrapped her arms around him? Sometimes she went crazy with want for him. He'd probably hold her for a minute then gently push her away. Maybe ask her to marry him... again. Dixie shivered, partly from cold. She couldn't take the risk.

"My mom..."

"You could invite her, too."

"Right." She snorted a laugh, the moment gone. "So we can all listen to her and your father yell and curse at each other? That would be a ton of fun for everyone, especially the kids."

"Okay, maybe not your mom."

"She's going on a cruise with her latest boyfriend, anyway."

Dan's gaze intensified. "So, you'll come? I'd hate to see you spend Thanksgiving alone. Or maybe I can tell my mom 'no,' and we can have a turkey here. I'll get a chance or two to see my sister over the weekend, anyway."

He'd give all that up for her? Sure, he would. He was just that kind of nice guy. Besides, he might not mind skipping his dad's bluster and his older brother's rudeness. At least his mom had been nicer the past few times Dixie had seen her, and Linnea was always lovely.

Dixie hadn't seen Linnea or her husband, Logan, since early summer. And since when was she afraid of Dave Senior? She straightened. "Yeah, sure, I'll come. Ask your mom what I can bring."

∽⌣

HAD DAN HEARD CORRECTLY? "Great! Don't worry about a thing. If Mom needs anything picked up, I'll provide it. You can be a guest."

Dixie rolled her eyes then opened her mouth as though to comment, but Henry grabbed at her jeans. "Mamama-ma?" Dixie scooped the little guy up and gave him a nuzzle. He giggled.

Whoa. Miracles never ceased. Even if that was just to get out of looking vulnerable, it was a win. "I can pick you up at two, if you like."

She set the toddler down. "I'll meet you there. That way, if things get nasty, I can escape."

Dan could hardly blame her for that. Nearly anything could set Dad off, and his language turned the air blue with the slightest provocation. But a miracle had happened once last summer when Dad actually apologized to his son-in-law for his language. Always respectful, Logan still felt free to call Dad out on his bullying nature. Even Dave Junior toned it down a bit around Logan.

Dixie reached for her coat, and Dan managed to snag it from the hanger before she did. He held it out as she slipped her arms into the sleeves. How his hands wanted to linger on her shoulders as he settled the faux fur collar in place.

"Thanks."

He blinked. *Thank You, Lord.* Maybe there was hope after all.

"Daddy!" yelled Mandy and, for once, Dixie didn't contradict her. "I'm a dancing angel!"

"Show me." He managed to remove his hands from Dixie instead of gathering her close, and turned to the little girl.

"Pretend there's music, okay?"

"What kind of music?"

"Um, a Christmas song about angels."

Dan wracked his brain. "How about *Angels We Have Heard on High?*"

"I think that's it." Mandy stuck one leg out behind her and held one arm high in front and the other behind her. "This is called arabesque."

"Okay. You've got good balance."

Mandy wobbled for a few seconds then lowered her limbs. "I can't do it without music. Because there's flying and jumping and stuff."

Dixie hadn't left yet. She stood beside him, jacket zipped up, and stared at her five-year-old.

He didn't have any Christmas music in the house, did he? And the moment would be lost if he hunted it up on YouTube and tried to choose a good rendition. Okay, fine. He'd sing it. He could remember the first verse, anyway. "Angels we have heard on high, sweetly singing o'er the plains. And the mountains in reply..."

Mandy dropped her hands to her hips. "Daddy, you know that song!"

"Sure, I do. Get dancing, baby."

He blocked Dixie's astonished stare from his periphery as Mandy resumed her position. He sang the first verse again and launched into the chorus. "Gloria, in excelsis Deo."

Mandy twirled around the living room, her brothers smart enough to stay out of her way.

Dan sang the *gloria* bit again, enthralled at the little girl's grace.

She swept a bow at his conclusion.

"Hey, baby, you're pretty good, you know that?"

She beamed proudly, her gaze bouncing off his and fixing on her mother's. "Did you like it, Mama? Did I do good?"

"Yeah, you're amazing. I didn't know they were teaching you to really dance."

Dan glanced at Dixie.

"Did you?" she asked. "I thought they were just doing a little kid pretend thing."

"I've never been to one of their church programs before, but Fran got Ava involved, and she takes dance at the academy, so I guess it shouldn't be a huge shock. The real surprise is how good this little missy is. We'll definitely have to get you into lessons next term, Mandy."

She clasped her hands together. "Yay! Thanks, Daddy."

Dixie didn't jump on it that time, either. "You did good, baby. I'll see you tomorrow." She turned for the door.

Dan opened it and followed her out onto the stoop. "Thanks, Dix."

She paused in the act of tugging her shoulder length blond hair out from behind the fur collar. "What for?"

"Making Mandy so happy."

"No biggie. She did good."

"It *is* a biggie. She really craves your approval. She soaked it right up."

"She's a good kid." Dixie cut him a glance. "I guess I need to say thanks to you, too."

He raised his eyebrows. "Oh?"

"You always seem to know how to please her. Who knew you could sing a Christmas carol all the way through?"

Dan shrugged. "There's more verses, I think. I might need to pick up a Christmas CD."

"I thought you were a Spotify guy."

"Yeah, but a CD would be easier for the kids."

Her eyes searched his face. "You're pretty awesome, you know that?"

He stilled. This usually meant she wanted something.

She stretched up and her lips brushed his. For just a moment, he gave in and gathered her close, intensifying the kiss. Dixie broke away first then bolted down the concrete steps and over to her car. She didn't even wave as she peeled out of the gravel driveway.

Dan stared after her, his lips tingling, his whole body yearning after her. She was such an exasperating woman but, no matter what Jacob advised, there was no way Dan could give her up. Call him a sucker for punishment, but he'd take whatever Dixie was willing to give him... without crossing any lines. If that made him look like a pathetic puppy, so be it.

He loved her. How was a guy just supposed to turn that off? He couldn't.

5

*D*ixie! It's so good to see you!" Dan's sister, Linnea, swooped in with her arms outstretched. "It's been ages. How are you doing?"

Dixie managed to survive a quick hug before stepping back. "Pretty good, thanks." All things considered, like how it was Linnea and Logan's fault Dan had chosen Jesus over Dixie last spring. It was hard to stay mad at his sister, though. She was a genuinely nice person in an annoying family and had really tried to be a friend to Dixie. Too bad she and Logan were enrolled at Edmonds Community College clear across the state.

Henry ran toward them, tripping over his feet and tumbling to the floor. The kid just bounced back up and finished the trek. Dixie swept him to her hip.

"I can't believe how much he's grown since summer." Linnea ruffled Henry's blond curls, but the little guy ducked away from her hand, nestling into Dixie's shoulder.

Whew. Maybe she'd survive a few hours with the Ranta family, after all. At least her kids loved her... most of the time. Dan wanted her here and had even brought the kids. It was a good idea to keep him happy occasionally.

Dan's mother poked her head into the entry area from the kitchen. "Linnea, can I get you to — oh. You're here, Dixie. I didn't hear you come in."

Dixie forced a smile. "Hi, Yvonne. I asked Dan what I could bring, and he said nothing."

Yvonne's smile looked as pained as Dixie's. "That's right. We've got everything covered. Won't you come in the kitchen?"

Yep. Anything that kept her out of the line of sight of Dan's dad and brother a bit longer was all right with her. She'd take either of them on toe-to-toe if she had to, but it upset Dan's gut — wait, since when did she care? She wasn't technically with him anymore, other than that they shared parenting.

"I just can't wait to move back to Spokane and put into practice the stuff we're learning in college!" Linnea gushed as she gestured Dixie to precede her. "Between Logan's business classes and my horticultural design and all Dan's hands-on experience with the company, we can offer more services than ever before."

"You're selling yourself short, aren't you?" Dixie set the wiggly toddler down as she leaned against the nearest cupboard. "You worked for Ranta Landscaping more years than Dan has."

Linnea sent a quick glance toward the living room door. "Just as a serf, though. Dan's been doing amazing things in the two years since he's taken the helm. Right, Mom?"

Yvonne shot her daughter a sharp look. "He seems to have kept it in the black, at least."

"Oh, come on, Mom! Give him some credit."

Her mother pursed her lips as she stabbed a fork in the potatoes. "He's lost some long-term customers."

"And gained new ones who want better ecological practices. I think he's way ahead. Don't you agree, Dixie?"

No way did she want into this conversation. "Um, sure." All she cared about was that he paid the rent, kept the kids clothed and fed, and was able to pay her something for watching the children. She'd hated to ask but, hey, a girl had expenses, and he seemed able to pay Fran, so why not her?

"Can you mash these, Linnea?" asked Yvonne.

"Absolutely."

"What can I do, Yvonne?"

Dan's mom glanced over, biting her lip. Had Dan really said his mom had asked him to invite Dixie? Because this was not a warm welcome. Mind you, there never had been. Dixie should be used to this treatment after nearly three years. Whoa. Had she and Dan really been together that long? Not that they were together, exactly. Dixie gave her head a shake.

"Can you get Dan or Logan to come carve the turkey?"

Her gut clenched. "Sure. Are they watching the game?" Dave Senior was bellowing at the TV, so things weren't going well in the other room.

Linnea pointed the masher at the patio door beyond the dining table. "They're out on the deck, talking."

Dixie nodded and circled the table, already set with a white linen cloth and Yvonne's prized china. Henry's high chair stood in the center of one side. Dan must have tossed it in the back of his pickup. She slid the glass door open a few inches and slipped outside, hearing the low murmur of men's voices around the corner.

"You still love her, then?" Logan's voice.

Dixie froze. The cold November wind with its hint of snow had nothing on her heart.

"I do." The anguish in Dan's voice clutched at her. "How do you just stop loving someone whose life is so entwined with yours?"

"I don't know, bro. And I know you're praying about it all. What has God shown you?"

Dixie eased the slider shut behind her as quietly as she could.

"I'm not sure. Guess that's obvious. Jacob said two wrongs don't make a right, and that makes sense. He said just because we have a son together doesn't mean I should marry her."

She knew she didn't like Jacob. How dare their neighbor judge her like that?

"She open to marriage at all?" asked Logan.

The silence lasted just long enough that Dixie could envision Dan shaking his head.

"Is she open to Jesus?"

Dan sighed. "Not that I know of. She's changed some in the past few months. I see glimpses of a softer side, but then those barricades whip right back up. All those men parading through her mom's life when Dix was a kid really messed her up. That's all the relationship she knows."

"I get it." Logan's chair creaked. "I didn't have a family to speak of, either. Like your little guy, my sisters and I all had different fathers. That was my biggest fear, really, that I'd let Linnea down. That my hang-ups were hereditary, and

I couldn't learn how to love one person for the rest of my life."

Huh. Why had she not known this about Logan? Because she'd never cared enough to look below the surface. He didn't affect her life.

Behind her, the glass slider rolled open with a loud rumble. "Dixie! There you are. Is one of the boys coming?" Yvonne called.

Dixie cringed as heat flared up her face.

The chairs around the corner creaked and Dan appeared. "Hey, Dix. What's up, Mom?"

Dixie licked her lips. "I was, um, sent to see if you or Logan would carve the turkey."

Dan's eyes narrowed at her, but she couldn't hold his gaze. Not when he knew she'd been eavesdropping.

Logan clapped Dan on the shoulder as his gaze toggled between them. "I've got the bird." He brushed past, followed Yvonne into the house, and slid the door shut.

Pretty sure Dan was the one with the turkey. Her.

⌒‿ɔ

"How long were you out here?" Dan couldn't help the sharpness in his voice. What all had he said to his brother-in-law? How would Dixie interpret — or, more likely, *mis*interpret — what she'd heard?

Her chin came up as she wrapped her arms tight around her narrow middle. "Should've known you'd be talking about me behind my back."

"It's not all about you, Dixie."

"It is when I hear my name." Her eyebrows peaked.

She had a point. Wouldn't he have paused to listen if he'd overheard her and a girlfriend talking about him? Sure, he would've. That might be the only way he'd ever know what she really thought of him, since she certainly wasn't telling him to his face.

Dan huffed a sigh.

"So, Jacob doesn't like me, huh?"

"I don't believe that's what I said. Or what he said, either."

"Oh, give up, Dan. It's the same thing, telling you marrying me would be a mistake. Probably he called it a *sin*. You Christians are all about pointing out someone's sins."

"Will you marry me? Because I'll go get a marriage license on Monday. I don't care what Jacob says." Did he care what *God* said? Yeah, of course, only God wasn't talking. Except for that verse one of the guys had pointed out at men's prayer breakfast a couple of weeks ago. Something about being unequally yoked with unbelievers. They'd been talking about it in the context of a business partnership, but Dan had read between the lines. The scripture had gone on to say, 'what partnership has righteousness with lawlessness?' Being as he didn't feel particularly righteous — and Dixie wasn't exactly lawless — he'd tried to shove the whole idea out of his mind.

"You'd go against your new religion?" She angled her head, face etched in disbelief.

"Dixie, I'd marry you in a heartbeat. You know that. You only need to say yes."

"Even if they say it's wrong?"

"What's wrong about a man and a woman committing their lives to each other? I love you, babe. I hate being apart." Basil's face drifted through Dan's memory, proof that even being together hadn't kept them from being apart. Dan stepped closer and reached for her hands, but she backed up a step.

"I'm never getting married. I'm not cut out for that kind of relationship. You know me." She offered a wan smile.

"I do know you." This time he advanced until she backed up against the stucco beside the patio door. He rested his hands on either side of her shoulders and watched while she nervously licked her lips. The sight turned his gut inside out. "Dixie," he said softly. "Please marry me."

Her head gave a tiny shake.

Dan leaned in closer and kissed her. He'd meant it to be a light brush, just enough to breathe a promise, but it wasn't enough. Not when her lips parted for his. He groaned, gathering her close as her arms slid around his neck. He deepened the kiss, yearning for her. *Lord, why is this so hard?*

"Take me home," she whispered between desperate, gasping kisses.

"Oh, Dixie." He pushed away an inch or two and tried to gather his thoughts.

"C'mon, Dan. You know you want me as much as I want you."

Problem was, he did. He really did. "I can't, babe."

This time it was she who ducked away, right out of his grasp. "Religion is kind of a killjoy, isn't it?"

He deserved that. "I want to do right by you. Treat you with the respect you deserve."

She laughed, but there was no humor. "I don't deserve respect. I'm not worth it. You know me better than that."

"I do know you. You're a wonderful woman, created by God for a purpose." The purpose of mothering her kids. Of marrying him. He couldn't say those things, though. He'd probably already said too much. He definitely knew he'd kissed too much, and that gave her power over him.

"Stuff it, Dan." The passion in her voice vanished completely. "I don't know why you didn't ditch me while you were ahead. Every other guy I hooked up with saw the truth much quicker than you did. You're blind or dense or both. I'm just a slut."

He heard the quiet desperation. "Babe, you're not *just* anything. Yeah, you've made some poor choices."

Her eyes flared in anger.

"What, you can say that, but I can't? I'm right there with you. I've made a lot of the same ones, in fact. But we were created for better, both of us. That's why Jesus came to earth. So He could redeem us. Give us a new hope and a new purpose."

Those arms wrapped around her belly again. "And you're stuck on your *old* purpose, thinking I'm worth your trouble. I'm not, Dan. Go do your lofty new thing. Jacob's right."

"He didn't mean it that way."

Dixie rolled her eyes. "Nice try. Ever since we first met, I knew you were too good for me. I almost felt guilty for dragging you down to my level, but I didn't let that stop me. I got pregnant on purpose, thinking I could hold on to you that way."

The words were a sucker punch, but they shouldn't have surprised him. He just hadn't realized she'd been quite that calculating. "You got your wish. You're stuck with me."

"I'm not." She shook her head. Her lips formed a thin

line, a far cry from the pliant welcome of a few minutes ago. "I'm no more stuck with you than with Brandon or Scott. They had no trouble walking away. So, go. Leave me to my own devices."

"Henry—"

"He'll be fine. In fact, you can have him. I'll take my other kids and get out of your hair. You'll thank me for that."

No. Never. "You can't, Dix—"

"Watch me."

"Babe, don't separate the kids." He closed his eyes, waves of nausea rolling over him. "We all need each other. The kids need their siblings. They need their mom. They need me, and I need them."

"I didn't have a father figure, and I turned out okay."

Dan managed to stifle a bitter laugh, but maybe not soon enough. "If you'd turned out okay, we wouldn't be having this conversation."

She drew herself to her full height, which wasn't saying much. "You're finally telling me what you really think of me."

There was no reasoning with her when she got this way. Everything he said would be used against him. Except this. "I'll tell you what I think of you."

Dixie's eyebrows rose as she stared back. "I can take it."

He gentled his voice as he searched her eyes. "I love you, Dixie Dawn."

"You can't." She stiffened.

Dan wouldn't have thought it possible. "You can't stop me from loving you."

"I bet I can."

The nauseous waves swelled into tsunami-strength breakers. Dan closed his eyes, waiting for the billows to calm, but that was going to take a while. Why had he challenged her? He knew better.

The heavy glass door rumbled on its rollers once, then again.

God! Where are You? I don't even know what to pray, what to ask. Please, please, please send healing. Cover Dixie with Your love. Cover me, too. I feel so empty.

In the distance, he heard her car start. That figured. If she was good at anything, it was running when she didn't get her way.

6

*W*here are we going, Mama?" Mandy asked from her booster in the back. "I'm hungry, and Grandma's dinner smelled so yummy."

"She's not your grandmother." Dixie yanked the steering wheel and turned east on Riverside. Dan's parents' house couldn't disappear out of her rearview mirror quickly enough. "We'll hit a drive-through in a few minutes."

"But—"

"No buts." Frantic ideas whizzed through Dixie's mind. She couldn't do this anymore. She just couldn't fit into Dan's life. Not as nanny to her own kids — wasn't that a joke? — and definitely not as his wife. He wanted too much. He stifled her.

Okay, all that aside, what other choices did she have? She needed to start thinking rationally. Taking Mandy with her when she bolted had not been rational. Her daughter had been sitting on the sheltered front step playing with her ballerina doll when Dixie stormed past. Impulse had taken over.

Wasn't that the story of her life? Think it. Do it. Worry about the repercussions later.

So... now what? She should have left Mandy with Dan. Because she wasn't coming back. Wait. She wasn't? What else was she going to do? She should have left Mandy... or taken Buddy, too. Henry was fine with his father. At least that was one kid she didn't need to worry about.

This was ridiculous. Could she really escape? Dan counted on her to watch the kids. Well, *her* kids. But he had a backup plan with Fran since Dixie was too flakey to show up on time every day. She'd been doing better but, yeah, she wasn't perfect. She wasn't wired to be perfect. Something inside her rebelled at the very thought, like a wild animal sensing a trap.

Being with Dan trapped her.

She needed freedom, but... the kids. So far, she'd dragged them with her, just like her mother had done with her. Dixie hadn't had much choice, other than abandoning them to the state, and she wasn't *that* bad. She had a choice now. Dan didn't want the kids separated. They were siblings, he said. Half-siblings.

And, wow, would they ever be better off without her. She was such a mess.

"Mama?"

The uncertain tilt of Mandy's voice chewed at Dixie's resolve. On the one hand, it would serve Dan right if Dixie took Mandy with her, but having a kid would only slow her down. Dan would fight for Mandy, but he wouldn't fight for Dixie.

She was going somewhere?

Yeah. She had to. Maybe Seattle. Basil Santoro was

there, and he wouldn't turn her away. They'd never had a chance to follow through before he'd run that police block and been arrested. He'd served his time for the DUI then left Bridgeview. He had such a big, nosy Italian family that Dixie could hardly blame him for escaping.

She knew what that need felt like. Right now, it consumed her. She needed away from her kids, away from Dan, and away from his religion. She was going to snap if something didn't change, and she was the only one who could make it happen.

"Mama, I'm hungry. Why are we at home? You said a burger, and I want a milkshake, too."

Dixie stared out the windshield as a bluster of wind spattered sleet against the glass. Without conscious thought, she'd pulled into Dan's driveway. She'd lived here, too, until he kicked her out after she'd left the kids for a couple of hours that day. Why was she here now? To pick up Mandy's clothes and toys before driving west?

Wrong choice. The kid didn't deserve to be hauled around by her loser mother. She'd be safe with Dan. Happy. Maybe if Dixie was right out of the picture, the kids would forget about her. After a while, Dan would be relieved. He wouldn't need to pretend to love her anymore. He'd find some other woman, a nice one who believed like he did, and marry her. The kids would have a new mother, not some crazy impulsive loser.

Why, oh why, had she told Mandy to come with her? She'd just wanted to control something, anything, but she shouldn't have. She was always doing the wrong thing.

Send Mandy inside for her things? Or leave her behind? Oh, God, what a mess she'd made of her life. Was still making. If God loved her like Dan said, why didn't He stop her? Prove Himself to her?

Dixie grimaced. That had been far too much like a prayer for her liking.

THE TV BLARED in the other room, the cheering a crescendo as Dan entered the house. He liked football as much as the next guy, but today, he couldn't care less. He'd taken a few minutes to pray, trying to quiet his mind and soul after Dixie's abrupt exit. He'd blown it. Again. He shouldn't have kissed her. Shouldn't have challenged her.

He was so tired of walking on eggshells for fear of setting her off.

The kitchen smelled homey. Mom had made a few apple pies, the cinnamon fragrance flirting with the robust aroma of golden turkey. For the moment, no one was fighting or yelling. The kids must be playing in the living room and keeping out of Dad and Dave Junior's way.

Dan took a deep breath and let it out slowly as he dragged the glass slider shut and allowed the cozy warmth to wrap around him after the chill of the back porch. The chill of Dixie.

Logan glanced over from the island where he massacred the poor bird, not that Dan could do a better job. "You okay?" he asked quietly.

Dan shrugged. "I've been better. She ran out of there like the devil himself was after her."

"Or God."

"Yeah, maybe."

Across the kitchen, Linnea scooped mashed potatoes into a china serving bowl. "Can you get the casseroles out of the oven, Dan? There are trivets for them on the table. We're about ready to eat."

Being useful would divert his spiraling thoughts. "Sure." He washed up at the sink, shifting out of Mom's way, then transferred the green bean casserole and the sweet potatoes to the table.

Dan studied the chair arrangements. He might as well pull Dixie's out of there and give everyone a bit more elbow room. It might draw less attention to her absence, because what he really didn't need was to explain to his dad and brother why she'd stormed out. He already knew what they thought of him for sticking by her.

He pulled out a chair, folded it, and shifted it to the hall closet. When he returned, Linnea was stacking Dixie's place setting. She glanced at him, sympathy in her eyes. "Sorry, Danny."

"Thanks. I really don't know what to do." Dan heaved a sigh. "I thought it would get easier. That she'd come around. It's just the opposite."

His sister touched his arm. "All we can do is keep praying. Logan and I do, every single day."

"Thanks. Me, too."

Linnea carried the dishes over to the china cupboard and put them inside while Dan closed the gap in the table settings. Mom set the gravy tureen down and analyzed the table.

"Looks good, Mom. Smells awesome."

"Thank you." She looked ready to say more but

appeared to think better of it. "Could you call everyone else for dinner?"

Great. That meant his brother could yell at *him* for missing part of the football game. It was hard to avoid with the games seeming to go all day. Dan walked into the living room. "Dinner time!"

Dad glared at him. Dave Junior ignored him.

Par for the course. Dan caught sight of the two little boys playing with blocks over by the window. Buddy wasn't usually this patient with Henry, so that was a win. "Come on. Buddy, wash your hands while I change your brother, okay? Dinner's ready."

"We'll come in a minute," said Dad.

Dan scooped the toddler, grabbed the diaper bag from the hall closet, and gave the kid a dry bottom before washing up again himself. He came back to the kitchen with Henry on his hip and Buddy by the hand.

The football game blared on.

Linnea pursed her lips and swept past him. "Dad! Dave! Dinner's ready. Time to shut the game off."

Better her than Dan. His sister had gotten all feisty in the past couple of years since Logan had entered her life. He'd been good for her.

Was Dan good for Dixie? Man, he tried to be.

"Where's Mandy?" Linnea asked as she turned back to the kitchen in the sudden silence.

"Good question." Dan thought for a sec. He hadn't seen her since shortly after they'd arrived. "Buddy, do you know? Was she playing with you?"

The little boy's nose curled. "She play dolly."

Yeah, she was obsessed with that ballerina doll. "Where did she go? Is she in one of the bedrooms?"

"Do'no."

Dan strapped Henry into the high chair. "I'll go find her." But Mandy wasn't in any of the bedrooms or bathrooms or behind the sofa. She wasn't in the basement or out in the backyard. Dan re-entered the dining room as Dad dropped into the armchair at the head of the table and Logan set the platter of turkey in the center. "Has anyone seen Mandy?"

Dave Junior glowered at him. "She took that stupid doll outside to play a long time ago."

Dan narrowed his gaze. "Outside where?"

His brother thumbed toward the front door.

"Excuse me." Dan strode to the front door and stepped outside. A blast of cold wind with hints of snow slammed him. Mandy wasn't there. Where could she be? She wasn't the kind of kid who wandered off or ran away. Unlike her mother.

Her mother.

He envisioned the scene. Mandy playing with her doll. Dixie storming past her, thinking of ways to prove to Dan that she could make him stop loving her.

His gut balled into a knot. She wouldn't.

Dan pulled out his phone. No messages. He tapped Dixie's number. It rang and went to voice mail. Twice. Three times, and then he left a message. "Dixie, where is Mandy? Call me, or I'll call the police." Maybe he should, anyway.

GUILT SWARMED Dixie as she threw her own clothes into a suitcase at her mom's apartment. Mom would be glad to have her out of there when she got back from her cruise. Dixie had been cramping her style. Mom would be somewhat less glad when she discovered her cash stash gone from the secret compartment under the jewelry box, but Dixie would pay her back once she got a real job. It would be okay.

There was far more guilt at leaving a five-year-old alone in the house down on Water Street. Dan would be back soon, though. He'd already called a few times and left a threat on Dixie's phone. He'd discover Mandy soon enough. And besides, though Dixie hadn't followed through on her promise of a burger and fries, she had made Mandy a baloney sandwich before locking the crying child into the house. Her kid was safe and fed.

Dixie wasn't going to forget her daughter's despair anytime soon. She was a terrible mother. Now she'd proven it beyond any doubt... like there'd been any.

Her phone rang again, and she glanced over at it where it lay, face up, on the bed. Dan again.

What was she doing? Dan was the best thing that had ever happened to her. He'd been her rock, her champion. He'd made her believe she could be a better version of herself. In a world where men came and went, he was different.

Even more different since he became a Christian. Not in a good way.

Dixie zipped the case shut and looked around the apartment. Had she forgotten anything she'd need? She had clothes. Her makeup. Cash, but who knew how long that would need to last? She should empty the fridge, too, to save money on food. She wouldn't want anything to go bad, since Mom wouldn't be back for over a week. Oh, and grab her beer. There was a collapsible cooler in the pantry. Done.

A few weeks ago, Mandy had earnestly told her a story she'd heard in Sunday School about a guy who'd run away from God and been swallowed by a whale. He'd had to say 'sorry' before the whale belched him back onto the beach so he could obey.

Maybe Dixie shouldn't be heading toward the ocean. Who knew if God had a whale for her, too? Of course, she wasn't as important as the guy in the story. God hadn't told her to do anything, so she wasn't technically disobeying.

Dan talked about the still small whisper inside a person being God's voice. The whisper that said Dixie was making a big mistake on top of her billion other ones. The whisper that said it wasn't too late to humble herself and make amends. The whisper that said God loved her even more than Dan did.

The whisper that was surely a figment of her imagination... and one she was good at ignoring.

7

*D*ixie stood in the apartment building's foyer with her hand on her wheeled suitcase and stared out at the white pellets angling from the sky. The sky had darkened in the half hour she'd been inside. The hint of snow had become a fulfilled reality.

Her temper had already cooled, and it settled further at the sight of the dark gray sky and sideways snow. It would be dark soon. Dark and ugly. Dan had put new tires on her car a few weeks ago, but that didn't mean she liked to drive in nasty weather. She should have thought of that before she stormed out of his parents' house. Dixie winced. Before she'd snatched her child and then abandoned her.

She'd made her bed and, as Mom always said, now she had to lie in it. Dan would never forgive her for what she'd done. What did it matter, though? She didn't want Dan.

Powered by the wind, a garbage can rolled across the parking lot and slammed into a light pole.

Dixie needed to think. Her plan had been impulsive. She thumbed on her phone and checked the Seattle weather. An early winter storm, rare on the coast, battered the city. She was not driving to Seattle. Not today. According to the forecast, not for a few days.

She couldn't stay at Mom's. Dan would find her for sure. She couldn't go back to the house on Water Street. Unless she got there before Dan and pretended she'd never left Mandy? But it had been too long.

On cue, her phone dinged. Yep. A text from Dan. *What were you thinking? Mandy's only five, Dix. You're lucky she's okay. Bawling her eyes out, but okay.*

Dixie blinked hard. She'd caused those tears. She was the worst mother. This time, she'd really gone and blown it. Dan wouldn't let her within five blocks of the kids ever again.

Where are you, Dix? We need to talk.

No. No, they didn't. She swallowed the lump in her throat. *You're better off without me. So are the kids. I'm sorry for everything.*

Babe, don't do anything rash. We love you. We need you.

If only love were enough, but it never had been and never would be. Dan panicked now, but soon he'd be relieved. He'd be a good dad to Mandy and Buddy. The State officials would grant him custody, wouldn't they? Or would they remove the kids into foster care?

Frost swirled in Dixie's gut. She couldn't let that happen, but she couldn't go back, either. Seattle looked out of the question. Besides, why would Basil welcome her? He'd never asked her to go away with him when he left last year. He hadn't sought her out the couple of times they'd happened to be in the same place after the night of his arrest.

Another text. *What are you thinking, Dixie?*

Dan's words echoed her own thoughts. It was a good question, and one she had no answer to. She'd watched a movie once where a bunch of hot cowboys eased mustangs into a wide funnel that ended in a small corral. The wild horses didn't know what was happening to them until it was too late, while the gate clanged shut behind them. Maybe a few got an inkling earlier on.

Those were the ones Dixie could identify with. There was a trap up ahead, but the walls angled in, forcing her down an ever-narrowing path. There was no one to blame but herself. She'd made every one of the choices that led to this moment in time.

She stared at Dan's text. Watched the bubble with the three dots in it, bobbing to indicate he was writing more.

No. She flipped to her contact list and found Tanisha's number. Tapped it.

"Dixie! Long time no hear. What're you up to, girl?" Loud music swelled in the background. Laughter.

"Hey, I need a place to crash for a few days. You got a couch?"

"Sure, anytime. You know that. You and Dan bailed me out more than once. Uh... I take it you're not with him anymore?"

The ding from an incoming text mocked that.

"Not exactly together, no. He got all religious on me."

The background noise quieted to a more distant pounding beat. "Daniel Ranta? No way. I'm so sorry. I thought he was a keeper."

Dixie swallowed hard. "Yeah, me, too. Anyway, he's got the kids, so it's just me who needs a spot if that's okay."

"Yeah, sure. I'm at a party at Billie and Jared's and don't figure on heading home until morning. Meet me there?"

Billie and Jared were together? Last Dixie knew, they'd each been with someone else. Things certainly changed. "Sure. Text me their address and I'll be over in a few. Can I bring anything?"

Tanisha laughed. "BYOB, of course."

Bring your own booze. She had that covered. "Okay. See you soon."

Dixie swiped over to her text app when it dinged again, but it was Dan again, not Tanisha.

Talk to me, babe.

Time was they'd have gone to a party like this one together. Dan could handle a fair bit of alcohol without doing something dumb, unlike Basil. Where Dixie didn't even need a stiff drink to be stupid. It came as naturally to her as breathing.

She wasn't answering Dan again until she was away from the places he could easily find her. And then she'd only answer so he'd quit pestering her and know he needed a different sitter for a while.

See? She was giving him fair warning. Wasn't that responsible of her?

⌒⌒

"She sure knows how to yank your chain." Dave Junior's nose curled in a sneer.

Dan shot his brother a glare as he settled into his chair at his parents' table, Mandy's arms still in a stranglehold around his neck. "Can we not do this in front of the kids?"

Dave Junior glanced at the others as though gauging support. Bullies always wanted someone to admire them.

"Good plan." Linnea arrowed a stern look at their older brother, who shrugged and mopped a dinner roll through the gravy on his plate.

It would have been too much to expect his family to await Dan's return for Thanksgiving dinner, especially since he'd had no idea how long he'd be when he left the house. If he'd been smart enough to take the boys, he wouldn't have bothered returning, but his sister was right. They'd been better off here with her. Buddy had polished off his plate, but Henry had picked at his until Dan appeared with Mandy. Now the toddler smeared mashed potatoes all over his high chair tray.

Mom bustled back to the table with two plates of food.

Really? She'd kept some warm? "Thanks. You didn't need to."

She glanced at Linnea. "Sure, I did. You just eat up now, and then we'll have pie."

Mom might not be a gourmet cook, but the spread was definitely better than anything Dan could come up with, especially with three hungry kids clinging to his legs. He shifted Mandy to his left knee so they could both eat.

"We waited for you to go around the table and say what we're thankful for," Linnea said.

Dan's fork paused halfway to his mouth. He remembered his sister had introduced this concept last year. They'd sure never done it growing up. And he had more to be thankful for than ever in his life. Even with Dixie's volatility? Yeah, he didn't much want to be vulnerable in front of his family, but what else was new? They all knew his business, anyway. "Sure. Want me to start?"

"Uh..." Beyond Linnea, he caught Logan's thumbs-up.

"I'm thankful for a lot of things." Dan cradled Mandy. "These amazing kids. A good year in the landscaping business. Meeting Jesus."

Dave Junior snorted.

Dan turned to his brother. "What're you thankful for, Junior?"

"Money."

Figured.

"Dad?" asked Linnea.

"Thankful to have a son who makes me proud."

Why did Linnea persist in giving their parents a venue for praising their firstborn? Because Dave Junior was about to pop his buttons, and it wasn't all because of the amount of turkey he'd no doubt put away.

"Anything else?"

Dad's gaze shifted around the table, lingering on Dan then Linnea before settling on Mom. "Thankful for your mother. And I guess I'm glad my ticker is doing better."

"Aw, thanks, Dave." Mom smiled at him. "We're glad you're back to health after that heart attack, too. I'm thankful to have all my chicks in the nest for Thanksgiving, and I'm glad everyone's getting along better than they used to."

Dan was *so* not going there. "How 'bout you, Mandy? What are you thankful for?"

The little girl chewed on her lip for a second before her eyes brightened. "Dancing. I'm going to be a Christmas angel!"

"You're all invited." Dan looked between his parents.

"Is it a school concert?" asked Mom.

"No, it's at Bridgeview Bible Church. Seven o'clock on the Sunday just before Christmas."

Dave Junior crossed his arms over his chest. "Not a chance."

Wasn't asking you. In earlier times, those words would have been verbal. Today, Dan managed to bottle them inside unspoken.

"Please, Grandma." Mandy batted her eyelashes.

"We'll see." Mom darted a glance at Dad then looked back at Mandy. "It sounds like you're having fun. That's good."

Mandy nodded before leaning over and poking Buddy. "What's your thank you?"

Buddy leaned against Dan's elbow. "My burfday. Daddy got me cars and a track. Cars go zoom." He demonstrated the speed around the loop, nearly toppling his water glass.

Mandy pivoted and pointed at Henry. "Say thank you."

"Ta Dadadada." He grinned as he splatted his pudgy hand into the potatoes. The kid had smeared gravy and sweet potatoes in his hair. Bath tonight. Maybe even before they left Mom and Dad's.

"Aw." Linnea sniffled. "He's so cute." She turned to Logan. "Your turn."

Logan slid his arm across the back of Linnea's chair and kissed her cheek. "Thankful for you, my love."

Dave Junior mimed a chokehold.

Logan grinned at him. "You're just jealous. Marriage to a great woman is a blessing not to be taken lightly. I'm thankful for new life in Jesus. For His forgiveness and love."

"Enough with the sermon, Dermott." Junior again.

"Your turn, Linnea." Logan's hand rubbed her shoulder, and she leaned against him.

Would Dixie ever trust Dan that much? Trust the Lord? His heart ached.

"I'm thankful there's only one more semester of college. It's been good, but I'll be glad to be done. And I'm thankful for each of you. My family." Her gaze traveled around the table, lingering on each of them. Even Junior. "And I'm super thankful for the joy and peace I have in Jesus. I wish you all knew it. It's amazing."

Mom shot another quick look at Dad.

Dan narrowed his gaze for a second. Were their parents starting to think about the Lord? Dan spent too much time wallowing in his own problems with Dixie and not time enough praying for others. Sharing with others. Memories of Al Santoro trickled through him. The fiftyish man had never wasted a moment he could share Jesus with anyone around him. His memorial service last year had been one of Dan's steppingstones. The man's entire life and death had nudged Dan toward faith.

Mom got up and began to clear the plates. Linnea and Logan retrieved serving dishes and glasses.

Dan ate the rest of his dinner, barely tasting it. He squeezed Mandy. "Eat up. Grandma made apple pie."

She swiveled on his knee and looked at him, tears puddling in her blue eyes. "Mama likes apple pie."

"I know, baby."

"Where did she go?"

"I don't know, but we'll find out later, okay?"

"I'm not hungry, Daddy. Mama made me a sandwich." She nestled against his chest.

His heart squeezed at the little girl's love. He was the only father figure she'd ever known, and he wasn't going to give Dixie another opportunity to take one of the children from him. That meant he had to fire her from childcare. Change the locks. Turn her loose.

No. He couldn't do that.

But this had been too close a call, with her taking Mandy then abandoning her. She'd obviously thought better of the responsibility, of the handicap a kid would present if she went back to her old lifestyle. Would she do that?

The churning in his gut said she would.

How could he pin her down long enough to get her to sign the kids over to him? Dan eyed his brother. Dave Junior was an attorney, but in criminal justice, not family matters. For this situation, Dan would need Peter Santoro's girlfriend, Sadie, a family lawyer. Dan had consulted with Sadie a few times before, so she had a pretty good grasp of the situation. This time, he needed to figure out what he could to become the children's legal guardian.

Would Dixie fight him on it or enable him? What about her unstable mother?

He'd give Sadie a call over the weekend and find out what his odds of success looked like. And check his phone in his jacket pocket in the front entry to see if Dixie had answered his last text.

Where had she gone?

8

*D*ixie had only thought she'd missed partying with her friends until she awoke on a carpeted corner of Billie and Jared's living room, anvils pounding her head and nausea spiraling her stomach. The sound of someone retching in the bathroom down the hall didn't help. Whoever that was would need to move over right quick.

She pushed herself to sitting and waited a few seconds for the dizziness to subside then tried to pick her way around the bodies sprawled on the floor. Oops. Tripped over Tanisha, but the other woman only shuffled over. Dixie made it to the bathroom as a big guy whose name she couldn't remember staggered out.

"Worst part of drinking," he mumbled as he shuffled past her.

Dixie cleared her own stomach. The guy was right. She was out of practice binging like this, thanks to trying to be a responsible mother for the past few months. Blast Dan and his stupid religion anyway. He'd driven her to this.

Someone pounded on the bathroom door as Dixie

splashed cold water on her face. She winced at her disheveled image in the mirror. Finger-combing her hair, she exited the small space and made her way to the kitchen, where the guy filled a mug from a giant urn. Someone had been thinking ahead.

He held it out to her. "Coffee?"

Dixie hated the stuff, but she needed the caffeine enough to drink it when required. She nodded, her skull pounding at the slight movement, as she slid into a chair at the dinette.

"Missed your name last night. I'm Seth." He dropped to the seat across from her, another mug in hand.

"Dixie." She took a sip of the vile liquid. The cure was as nasty as the hangover. That alone should be enough to keep her sober.

"Who invited you?"

What was with the twenty questions? "Tanisha. We go way back."

"Haven't seen you around the gang before."

She tried to focus on his tanned skin and dark hair. She didn't remember him any more than he seemed to remember her. "We moved across the city last year."

Seth's eyebrows peaked. "We?"

"My boyfriend and me. We split, though."

"Maybe his loss is my gain."

She rolled her eyes, even that motion painful. Who hit on someone with bedhead, bloodshot eyes, and puke-tainted breath? Dixie winced, remembering she'd been that desperate a time or two. Never again. She took a long sip of the thick brew then met the guy's gaze. "Don't think so. I'm gonna be single for a while."

Seth shrugged. "Can't blame a guy for asking."

If her brain wasn't misfiring, she probably could, but it took too much effort to think.

Billie entered the kitchen in sweats, went straight to the urn, and poured a coffee. She glanced between them before settling on Dixie. "Hey, hon. Haven't seen you in ages. How's Dan? The kids?"

From the corner of Dixie's eye, she caught Seth shifting away. Just as well, really. "We split. Dan's got the kids."

"Huh. Thought you guys were in it for the long haul."

Whatever that meant in their crowd. "Nearly three years."

"What happened, if you don't mind me asking? He didn't beat you, did he? Never thought he was the sort."

Dixie shook her head. "No. He's on a Jesus kick."

Sympathy flooded Billie's eyes. "I'm sorry, hon. Religion can really mess things up."

"You're telling me." Except Dan had turned into a nicer version of himself since his conversion. A man she was even more attracted to. If only he hadn't decided sleeping with her was a *sin*.

"Don't even start with me about religion," Seth muttered.

Dixie's eyebrows raised as she stared at the guy. "Been burned?"

"It's all great while you're in it. It's kind of a high, with all that love, joy, peace."

She'd seen that in Dan.

"But then when you realize it's not all it's cracked up to be, it's an ugly crash." He slammed the table, and Dixie jumped. "Euphoria's gone. The world is nastier than it ever was before." Seth lurched to his feet. "I need a drink. You?"

Dixie shook her head. She'd definitely had enough for now. Maybe forever, if she could hold onto how grim she'd felt half an hour ago. An occasional beer or drink with dinner? No problem. She'd been doing that for years — minimally while pregnant. But she hadn't gotten this soused in eons. She didn't even want to think about how much she'd guzzled last night.

Yeah, she'd arrived well after the party had started, but Billie had still met her at the door, told her where to hang her keys, and informed her no driving, no exceptions. A good hostess, right down to having the huge coffee urn prepped for the morning after.

Billie slid into Seth's vacated seat as Tanisha wandered into the kitchen. "Dan's got the kids? How'd that happen? Only the baby is his, right?"

"Yeah. Henry's eighteen months now." Dixie sighed. "It's a long story, but he's good with the kids, and they love him."

Tanisha glanced over from the urn. "Aren't you going to fight for them?"

"Why should I?" Dixie met her friend's gaze.

"Because...?" Billie lifted both hands.

"Look at me. I'm a mess. The kids are better off without me. He can give them everything I can't. A real home. Stability. Regular food."

Tanisha snorted. "He can't give them a mother's love."

"Not that I can." Dixie rolled her eyes. "Not really. Did you miss the part where I'm a mess?"

Billie eyed her over the rim of her coffee cup. "Do you love your kids, Dixie?"

"Of course, I do. That's why I know leaving them with Dan is best for them."

"My mom abandoned me when I was a baby." Tanisha sipped her coffee, closing her eyes for a second as she leaned back against the counter. "I don't think anything can mess up a kid more."

"But I'm not good for them. I know it. They'll forget about me in time. Maybe Dan will marry someone who'll take my place." Just the thought tightened a new band around her skull.

"They won't forget," Tanisha said quietly. "No one can take your place."

"But—"

"She's right, you know," Billie put in. "I was shuffled around in foster care, too. Had some decent placements, all things considered, but the only thing I really wanted was my mom. Even after I couldn't remember her face."

Dixie sighed. "You haven't convinced me. My mom kept me, but I didn't feel safe or loved considering the parade of men through our apartment."

"Hit on?" asked Billie.

"Not the way you're thinking. Just felt vulnerable. Afraid." And determined to control her own sexual destiny, not be taken advantage of by some leering jerk three times her age.

"You say you love your kids." Billie took a sip. "Why?"

"That's a dumb question."

Tanisha shook her head. "I don't think so."

Of course, they'd stick together. "Because they're my kids."

"Not because they're cute, or talented, or something else?"

"Of course not. I don't need more reasons."

"How can another woman ever give them that?"

"But—" Dixie snapped her mouth shut.

"Yeah, I agree." Billie nodded. "You need to either get back with Dan, or take the kids with you. I'm not even kidding when I say they need you more than anything else."

Dixie sliced her hand through the air. "Enough. I'm not going back. Did you miss the part about him finding religion? He figures we need to get married, or we can't live in the same house. Definitely no hanky-panky."

"He asked you to marry him?" Tanisha asked incredulously.

"A dozen times."

"And you turned him down?"

Dixie rolled her eyes. "A dozen times."

"I don't get you, hon." Billie eyed her. "He's a good guy. The kids are safe with him. He's got a good job. He wants to marry you. Don't let a little religion get in your way."

"Yeah, I thought you meant he'd decided you weren't good enough for him."

"I'm not. Don't you get it?"

Her friends exchanged glances then Billie shook her head. "You've got everything you ever wanted offered to you on a silver platter. Just take it."

Dixie gulped the now-lukewarm coffee and pushed to her feet. "It's not that easy." Not when it came with an extra — Dan's newfound faith.

DAN HELD the door for his friends. "Come on in. Can I get you anything to drink? Coffee? Tea? Pop?"

Peter ushered his girlfriend in with a touch to her lower back.

Sadie shrugged off her coat into Peter's hands and grimaced. "I'd better stick with water. I'm off sugar, and I hate coffee without loads of flavored creamer."

She'd lost a lot of weight since Dan had given her a landscaping quote last spring. If ditching sugar had made the difference, he sure didn't want to be responsible for sabotaging her.

Peter chuckled. "I'll take a cola. I've cut back a lot, but I'll still indulge."

"So long as you keep your boyish figure." His girlfriend patted his flat belly.

A diamond glistened on Sadie's hand. Dan swallowed hard. "Looks like congratulations are in order."

Sadie wiggled her fingers, a soft smile on her face. "Yep. He finally got around to asking me."

"Hey, it's not like that!" Peter protested. "And you're the one who insists the wedding won't be until Thanksgiving. Which happened to be two days ago, so you mean an entire year."

"You're the one who's got a super busy job from spring through fall and can't take time off."

Peter kissed her cheek.

Dan turned away, heading for the kitchen. Let the lovebirds come when they were ready. Yeah, their engagement wasn't a huge shock, but on the heels of Dixie's disappearance, it only twisted the knife in his own gut. Last week he could have pretended he'd win Dixie over any day. Now? Not so much.

He dumped ice into three glasses and filled one with water. By the time he'd poured cola into the other two, the happy couple stood hand-in-hand beside the counter. Dan passed over their drinks then picked up his own.

Understanding flickered in Sadie's eyes. "You had some questions?"

"Yeah. Let's go have a seat in the living room." Dan glanced up the staircase as he passed it. He hadn't heard a peep from the three of them for nearly an hour. He'd just as soon they didn't overhear. Mandy, especially. She was still a clingy wreck from Thursday.

Sadie took a sip of water then set her glass down. "Tell me what's happening."

The visit between friends had just turned into a client's consult with his family attorney. "I can't expect you to keep handling my affairs for free, Sadie. Would you please send me a bill?"

She quirked a grin. "You can't afford me. Don't worry about it. If we incur any filing fees, I'll bill you, but advice? That stays pro bono."

"Thanks. I don't deserve friends like you." His gaze toggled between the couple then sighed. "Everything's a mess."

"Last I knew, you were living in this house, and Dixie was coming over to watch the kids most days while you were at work. Is that still true?"

"It was until Thanksgiving. She came to my parents' house for dinner at my request. I'm not sure why she agreed. I mean, her mom's out of town, and my sister's always been kind to Dixie, but I thought she'd turn me down. Stupid me. I thought it meant something when she came."

Sadie nodded. "So, what happened?"

"Logan and I were talking outside, and she overheard me tell him Jacob told me I shouldn't marry her. That two wrongs don't make a right." Dan scrubbed his hands through his hair. "He's got a point, I guess."

"What was her response?"

He shook his head. "I told her I loved her and asked her to marry me, for probably the twentieth time. I don't care what Jacob says. Dixie's the mother of my son, and I want a whole family."

"And then?"

"She told me I couldn't love her, and I said she couldn't stop me." He closed his eyes, remembering. "She said she bet she could. And then she left me on the porch and drove away. I didn't realize she'd taken Mandy for probably fifteen or twenty minutes. I thought she was in the other room playing with the boys."

"Oh, no. Is Mandy okay?"

"Dixie thought better of her decision and left Mandy here at the house. Made her a sandwich and locked her in. Then took off again, on her own. Her car's not at her mom's, and she's not answering my calls. She's replied to a couple of texts."

Sadie closed her eyes. "Poor kid. Mandy must be devastated."

"She is. All she wants is her mom. Meanwhile, she'll barely let go of me."

"Guess she's afraid you'll disappear, too." Sympathy

laced Peter's voice.

"It might be what's going through her mind. Seems the only way to convince her is to be here for her."

Peter's eyebrows rose. "Twenty-four seven?"

"I know. I can't do that and run a business. That's another big problem, but it's not something you can help me with. I hadn't thought about the fact that I get up at two or three in the morning when there's been a snowfall so I can get driveways and parking lots cleared before business hours begin. That was no big deal when Dixie and I were together. She was here when the kids woke up. It all worked. Now I need someone who lives in." He gave a sharp laugh. "Obviously not her or another woman."

Peter cringed. "Yeah. I can see that's a big problem. Good thing Thursday night's snow turned into rain and didn't accumulate."

"Right, but the forecast calls for snowfall by next weekend, so I need a solution soon. It just completely spaced my mind how Dixie's and my separation — and the kids living with me — would affect a once-minor thing like that." Dan gave his head a quick shake. "Anyway, that's not your problem, and nothing I shouldn't have seen coming."

"Is it time for you to file for custody?" Sadie asked quietly.

Man, he did not want to go here. He stared at the attorney. "It feels like I'm giving up on Dixie."

She met his gaze but said nothing.

"I guess... I guess I *am* giving up. I can't keep living like this. Not just me, but the kids. It's so hard on them. This thing with Mandy — it just kills me to see how sad she is."

Sadie nodded. "Okay. Here's what we're going to do..."

9

Beggars can't be choosers.

Dixie shoved aside thoughts of leisurely days playing with her kids as she tugged the way-too-short uniform over her backside. She couldn't mooch off Tanisha indefinitely.

Just be thankful Kristoff needs a barmaid again. Don't think about the leering drunks.

Since when? She'd enjoyed working here before, hadn't she? Why did the thought of the upcoming shift make her so uncomfortable now? She could handle the men. Contrary to what it looked like — three kids with three different partners — she'd only said *yes* when she felt like it. No dude would get past her defenses tonight, either, or any night she had to work in this godforsaken job.

Hand holding her mascara wand, she stared at herself in the mirror. *Godforsaken?* Didn't that mean there was a God somewhere with places He frequented? Like church, maybe. But Dan had talked about God being everywhere and seeing everything. Loving everyone.

Dan had rocks in his head. God didn't hang out at Kristoff's, that was for sure. Dan didn't, either. Not anymore. Between taking over the family business and then finding Jesus, Dan had turned into an even better version of himself. There was no chance he'd show up in the bar while she was working.

No, he was home with three little kids tucked into bed. Probably had some music on. Maybe watching a documentary on Netflix or doing paperwork for the company. Dan, the responsible adult.

Well, Dixie was responsible, too. That's why she'd landed herself a job. Dan had rescued her from all this a couple of years ago, but he'd changed, and she'd pushed him past the breaking point.

She tucked the makeup bag away and gave herself a big smile in the mirror. It looked a little fake, but it was the best she could muster at the moment.

Time to work.

THREE KIDS STRAPPED into their car seats at the curb, Dan strode up the walkway to his landlady's house, check in hand. He rang the doorbell and kept an eye on the truck while he waited.

The door swung open, and Marietta Santoro stood before him. The neighborhood matriarch must be pushing eighty, if she wasn't already there, but she stood plump and erect, her gaze flicking from the truck to him. "Danilo."

"I've brought my rent check, Mrs. Santoro." If only she'd be willing to accept an e-transfer, but no.

"Grazie." She accepted the paper from his hand. "How are the little ones?"

"Uh, good. Everything's good." He probably shouldn't lie to the woman, but he couldn't go into all the details with every random person he ran into.

"I hear Dixie has disappeared, no?"

So, Marietta already knew. "She has."

She stepped back and beckoned. "I have coffee. Cookies for the children. Bring them in."

Dan hesitated. Did he have time for this? He had more phone calls to make in his desperate search to find a male overnight sitter. Spokane had gotten by with a few mild snow skirmishes, but that was about to change, and Dan needed that sitter in place.

"Come."

"Okay. Thank you." Ten minutes wouldn't make that much difference. He jogged down to the truck and unbuckled Henry. "Come on, you guys. Mrs. Santoro has cookies for you."

Buddy's face brightened, and Mandy did a wiggly dance as she unbuckled her booster. "I like Tieri's bisnonna."

Dan hadn't realized the kids had anything to do with Marietta when he wasn't around. Did that account for the woman's knowledge about Dixie? Maybe, but in a close-knit community like Bridgeview, the news had likely spread like wildfire.

He ushered the kids into Marietta's Mediterranean-style home with its rounded stucco arches then set Henry down and bent to unzip his parka. "You kids behave, you hear?" he said in a low voice. "And say thank you."

Mandy nodded. Buddy kicked off his boots, showing no sign of hearing.

Dan grasped the four-year-old's shoulder. "Buddy?"

"I be good."

That would have to do. They followed Marietta over large terra cotta pavers into the huge kitchen at the back of the house, with its creamy cabinetry and warm granite counters. Dan pointed the kids at wrought-iron stools beside the island, and they obediently climbed up.

Marietta opened a cookie jar shaped like a round chef, complete with handlebar mustache, and moved a handful of cookies to a plate. "Here, eat." She set the plate between Mandy and Buddy.

Buddy's eyes grew round as he grabbed a treat with each hand. When had the kid last met homemade cookies? Dan had no clue.

"Grazie, la bisnonna," Mandy said primly.

Dan stared at her, trying to translate. *Thank you, great-grandmother?* Since when could his kid speak any Italian? Huh. Must be Fran's doing.

Marietta smiled and patted Mandy's hair.

Well, maybe the child had paved the way to a pleasant visit. Dan had a hard time forgetting that Marietta had been reluctant to rent out one of her houses to a common-law couple. Only her son Ray's encouragement had made her agree in the first place.

She poured two coffees and beckoned at the nearby table. "Come. Sit."

Still holding Henry, Dan did as he was told.

Marietta poured milk for the kids then brought cookies

to the table before taking a seat herself. "Now you tell me how it is with you."

Dan hesitated. How could an old woman like her help him? Wasn't she doing more than her share by allowing him and the kids to have a home? But she did know everyone in the community, and she certainly knew how to pray.

He took a sip of deep, rich coffee then met his landlady's dark eyes. "I have a problem."

She raised her eyebrows. "Si?"

"We're going to get snow soon, and that means plowing in the early morning hours. If I can't find an overnight sitter — male, obviously — I'll have to hire all the plowing out or cancel contracts." What could he do over the winter for income if he canceled contracts? When Dixie returned and married him, how would he get the work back? *If* she did. He sighed.

Marietta nodded. "You have three bedrooms."

Of course, she knew. It was her house. "I'd have to let the sitter sleep in my room, I guess. Means the sofa for me, but there's not much way around that."

"Unless you move the children together."

Hmm. Dan glanced over at Mandy and Buddy, who'd packed away most of the cookies on the plate. He and Dixie had separated the wooden bunk when they'd moved into this house. Would it be okay to put them back together? There'd be room in the boys' room for Mandy that way.

She'd hate it. Or would she?

Then her room could go to the sitter. The sitter he still needed to find. "That's an idea."

"Have you met Antonio? He is the son of my son Matteo, who lives in Idaho, but Antonio comes to

Bridgeview to open an Italian restaurant. My sons say Antonio should live with me for now." She grimaced. "They think I cannot live alone anymore, but they are wrong. Maybe he could live with you."

"Antonio?" Dan wracked his brain, trying to remember every Santoro he'd met. There were a lot of them. He knew Peter, Alex, and Basil the best. Dan had even lived in Alex's basement suite when he and Dixie first separated. But he couldn't place Antonio. "Wouldn't your grandson want to stay with his cousins?"

Marietta swept her hand. "Alex rented out his suite to college students. Besides, my family is convinced Antonio should stay with me." She narrowed her gaze at Dan. "You would do me a great favor to give him a place to live. My sons would surely see you need him more than I do."

Conniving old woman. Dan couldn't stop his chuckle. "Tell me more about him."

"He comes tomorrow from Arcadia Valley. He's been working at his mother's brother's restaurant there for a couple of years, but his uncle Franco has found him a building to renovate here for his own restaurant. He is a fine *cuoco* — chef — with much training and experience for a young man of twenty-seven years."

Dan's mind raced. Could he offer a stranger not a babysitting job, but a home, even temporarily? But if the man's grandmother vouched for him, a guy with this much ambition, it might buy Dan some time. "I'd like to meet him."

"Bueno. I will send him over when he arrives. My sons cannot fault this arrangement." Marietta nodded decisively. "Have a cookie."

Dixie stared at her ringing phone. An unknown number, so it wasn't Dan. With the number of resumés she had out, she couldn't afford not to answer. "Hello, Dixie speaking."

"Dixie! I'm so glad I reached you."

No way. She should've at least scanned the area code. "Hi, Linnea."

"How are you, sweetie? We've been so worried."

"I'm fine. Thanks."

"Have you been in touch with Dan?"

Dixie's jaw clenched as she stared out the smudged window, the only view that of the equally dilapidated high-rise across the street. "Not exactly." Dan texted her every day with a story about the kids, or telling her he missed her. She'd answered a couple of times, but she'd rather he didn't expect a response to his every summons.

"Aw, he misses you."

"Look, Linnea—"

"I know it's not really any of my business, but I love my brother, and I adore the kids."

Dixie made a mental note of who was *not* included in that list.

"And I really care about you, too. I feel terrible that we weren't able to stay in Spokane longer last weekend, because I wanted to spend some time with you, but with that storm coming in, Logan wanted to get back."

Not that Dixie would have accepted a cozy chat. Although... in times past, she'd begun to warm to Dan's sister. She was a sweet woman. But, hey, another Christian. "I've been busy."

Linnea laughed. "That's great! Sounds like you've landed on your feet, then."

Whatever that meant. "Well, I found a job." Drat. Dixie zipped her lips. If she told Linnea where, she'd tell Dan, and then he'd show up at the bar, all caveman, to haul her away.

In some ways, she wouldn't mind. Where once she'd flirted right back at the customers, she couldn't quite bring herself to do it now. She shifted away from their familiar touches. And, yes, her tips suffered from it.

"Good for you. Where are you working?"

"Look, if Dan put you up to this—"

"Oh, no. Of course not."

Right. Dixie doubted that. "I'm fine, okay? You don't need to worry about me. Dan and the kids are better off without me."

"Oh, sweetie, is that what you're telling yourself? They're not, you know. Dan says Mandy cries herself to sleep every night, begging for her mama."

Guilt stabbed Dixie, a shaft deep in the heart. "I can't be the mother she needs. I just can't." Somehow, the pain had bubbled out in her voice.

"I'm sure praying for you, Dixie. God wants you to come home. I don't mean to Dan — although maybe that, too — but it's really God you're running from. That reminds me of a story in the Bible—"

A sharp laugh came out of Dixie's mouth. "I live far enough inland I don't need to worry about some whale getting me."

"What?" Linnea chuckled. "Oh, you're thinking of Jonah. I meant the prodigal son. It's a story Jesus told in the book of Luke, about a man who took his inheritance and squandered it all until he was destitute and hungry. Then he remembered his father loved him and would welcome—"

"Nice story," Dixie cut in. "My mother's a little less forgiving, and Dan owes me nothing. Listen, I have to go. Thanks for calling." She tapped the screen to end the call.

She should've known Linnea was only looking for a way to preach at her. Everyone was so judgmental, so certain they knew what was best for her. Well, they didn't. Linnea hadn't lived her life, hadn't made the decisions Dixie had. She'd made plenty of bad choices besides the ones that had resulted in three small humans.

Dixie's heart ached. She would never have believed she could miss those kids this much. It had only been a week since she'd last seen them. Henry with his wispy baby curls and sweet babbling. Buddy with his exuberant giggles and more energy than should be legal. Mandy, sobbing as Dixie hardened her heart and locked her in the house.

Even knowing Dan would be there in minutes, she shouldn't have done that. She knew it now. She'd known it then, too, but her anger had compelled her. The nerve of their neighbor telling Dan marrying Dixie was wrong.

Not that she wanted to marry him.

Well, yes, she did. She ached for him. Not just his tender kisses, but the reality of being a family. Why was she so stubborn? Why couldn't she just give in and marry the guy? He hadn't even demanded she love God or go to church. He'd take her as she was.

She wasn't good enough for him, though. Not good enough to be a wife or a mother. She'd made such a mess of everything.

Dixie thought again of wild horses being driven toward

a corral. She could almost hear the gate creaking and the latch clanging. What would happen when she was truly cornered?

Linnea had mentioned the prodigal son. It sounded vaguely familiar, like Dixie had heard the story somewhere before. What made that guy change his direction and go home?

She thumbed open her phone and searched. The story popped up. Yikes, the guy had resorted to eating pig slop. That was a whole lot worse than dumpster diving, and Dixie hadn't even had to do that yet. Not this time around, thanks to Tanisha and Kristoff.

Dixie kept reading. Then she got to the bit where the father said, *'Let's prepare a great feast and celebrate. For this beloved son of mine was once dead, but now he's alive again. Once he was lost, but now he is found!'* She stared at the words before reading a little further. *And everyone celebrated with overflowing joy.*

Well, wasn't that beautiful? A touching moment that got her right in the feels? The story even caused a few tears to gather in her eyes.

She didn't have a father like that, one who'd love her unconditionally. She'd only met the man who'd sired her a couple of times, years ago. He definitely hadn't been the staying kind.

Dan would be, if she only let him. She knew that, but she also knew Dan wasn't enough.

And everyone celebrated with overflowing joy.

If only it were real, and not a fairy tale.

10

The doorbell rang, and Buddy raced to the door, sliding on his sock feet. "Mama here!"

Dan's heart clenched. "Remember what I said. Only a grownup may open the door." He strode into the entry.

"But Mama!"

If only. "It's not your mother." Dan scooped Buddy into his arms as he turned the knob.

A young man stood on the doorstep, obviously a member of the Santoro clan with his dark hair and startling blue eyes. An easy grin stretched across his face as he held out his hand. "You must be Dan Ranta?"

"I am." Dan gave the guy's hand a firm shake. "Antonio Santoro, I assume."

"Tony." The other man laughed. "Only my nonna insists on my legal name."

"Well, come on in. This is Buddy, who just turned four." Oh, no. Dan had forgotten to ask Marietta whether this guy was comfortable with kids... but she wouldn't have suggested the arrangement if he wasn't. Right? Although, knowing the older woman, he wouldn't put it past her if it offered the results she wanted.

Buddy stared with open curiosity as Tony wrinkled his nose and grinned at him.

"This is Mandy. She's in kindergarten." Dan motioned to the little girl as she carried a glass of water to the table. "Mandy, say hello to Tony."

"Hi." She studied him then turned back to Dan. "Henry has a poopy diaper."

Dan stifled a groan. Of course, he did. Timing was everything. He slid Buddy to the floor and grabbed the stinky toddler. "Sorry. I'll be right back."

When he returned a few minutes later, Tony was seated in the middle of the sofa with a kid snuggled on either side, reading *The Very Hungry Caterpillar* in an expressive voice. "...but he was *still hungry!*"

Buddy giggled. Huh. He hadn't smiled a lot in the past week since his mom had disappeared. Maybe Tony was a godsend after all.

"More story!" Buddy scrambled off the sofa.

Tony glanced over at Dan. "Maybe in a bit. I came to visit with your daddy."

Mandy surged to her feet and placed both hands on her hips. "Mama says he's not our daddy. Just Henry's."

And that one had been acting out all week, pinballing from being super needy to standoffish. Dan's heart ached for her. How was a guy supposed to handle the situation? And, if he did win custody and he and Dixie stayed separated, how on earth was he going to see Mandy through her teenage years? She didn't need hormones to be a handful.

Tony's gaze bounced between them, but he stayed quiet.

Smart man. No doubt his grandmother had briefed him on the situation.

"Let me show you around upstairs," Dan said. "Then the kids can get ready for bed while we talk."

Buddy scowled and crossed his arms. "No bedtime."

Dan ruffled the little boy's soft curls. "But it is. You want to show Tony your stuffed tiger?"

"Okay." Buddy scrambled up the stairs. "Come see."

"I know it's a little backward." Dan led the way up. "We haven't talked about any of the details, but I'd rather have that conversation after the older two are tucked in bed. So, forgive me for being vague in front of them."

He pointed into the first bedroom. "This is Mandy's current room. Beside it is the boys' room. These can be... ah... consolidated. The beds form a bunk."

Tony nodded, peering into one space then the other.

"Here's the hall bathroom. And then the master bedroom is a little bigger with its own bath."

Buddy shoved his tiger at Tony's leg. "See?"

The man squatted and touched the stuffie's head with a gentle finger. "He's so fuzzy. What's his name?"

"Tiger."

"A tiger named Tiger. At least we won't forget his name, right?"

The little boy looked at him uncertainly then dashed back into his room.

"Get your pajamas on, Buddy," Dan called.

"No want to."

"It's time, anyway. Mandy, you, too."

She scowled at him but went into her room and shut the door rather firmly.

This wasn't the moment to reprimand her. Dan turned back to Tony as they descended the steps. "Downstairs is mostly what you saw. Kitchen, dining space, living room. A laundry room with a half bath. An office too small to be a bedroom. Outside we've got a decent covered patio and fully enclosed backyard. Great place for the kids to play." He felt like a real estate agent trying to sell the property.

Keeping Henry with him, Dan hurried through tucking the older ones in bed, aware of a virtual stranger sitting in his living room. It seemed crazy to offer a home and job to someone he didn't know, but he was fresh out of options. He had to trust the guy, though. Had to trust Marietta's assessment of her grandson.

Tony sat at the kitchen table jotting into a notebook when Dan returned. The few dirty dishes had been washed and stacked in the drain rack, and the living room had been tidied, not that it had been messy. Dan had been home all day, every day, for the past week, with little else to do besides keep things picked up.

The other man looked up, set down his pen, and leaned back in his chair. "Nonna mentioned you needed someone to live in for early morning childcare?"

No beating around the bush. That could only be a good thing, right? "It's true. Did she also tell you all about me?"

Tony chuckled. "Maybe. Why don't you tell me what you think is pertinent?"

Dan set Henry down, and the little boy toddled off to clench a toy car in each hand. "So, Mandy's right. I'm not her dad, hers or Buddy's, just Henry's. Dixie Wayling is the mother of all three kids. We were together for a few years. Marriage was never a priority until I became a Christian about six months ago. Dixie... isn't interested in God. We separated, and she stayed here with the kids until she left them to go drinking one day. Then I moved back in and kicked her out. That was in July."

"God has a way of upending our lives," Tony said quietly.

"Sure does." Dan scrubbed a hand through his hair. "It's worth it, totally, but it's come with a fair share of challenges. Anyway, I took over my dad's landscaping business a couple of years ago. Dixie came here most days to watch the boys while I worked. When she didn't show, I dropped the boys off at Fran Amato's."

"My cousin Fran. Our dads are brothers."

"Right. Of course. She's great, and Buddy and Luca play well together. Only two things have happened recently to complicate things even further. One is that Dixie's gone." Dan lowered his voice and glanced toward the stairs, hoping the silence meant the kids were asleep, or at least in bed and not eavesdropping. "She's messed up. My lawyer is helping me file for custody."

"My cousin Peter's fiancée?"

Dan chuckled. "You really are related to half of Bridgeview. Yes, Sadie. She's been very helpful all through this mess. Anyway, the other thing I should have seen coming. In the winter, when lawns are dormant, Ranta Landscaping takes snow-removal contracts. We have a number of longstanding customers. The thing that I wasn't paying attention to was the timing. I need to be out there in the middle of the night if it's snowing, clearing parking lots and driveways before the morning commutes. The past couple of years, Dixie's been here with the kids, so I didn't need to think about them."

Tony rested his elbows on the table and studied Dan. "Nonna respects you, and so do my cousins."

"She does?" Dan wanted to be upset at being talked about behind his back, but this was interesting info. "She didn't want us as renters because we weren't married, but her son—"

"My uncle Ray talked her into it." Tony laughed. "I may never have actually lived in Bridgeview before, but I've spent a lot of time here, and I'm close with my family."

"At any rate, that's my predicament. I don't have many decent options. Hire a sitter whom I can call at three a.m. to come over if I need to plow. Have the kids spend the night at Fran's, or somewhere else, any nights it looks like snowfall is an option, or..." He spread his hands.

"Or have someone like me move in, someone who can roll with it."

"Yeah. Or hire another guy to run the third Bobcat and take the financial hit, which has looked like the best option until now."

Tony leaned back into his chair. "About me. I graduated from culinary school in Seattle, worked in a couple of top restaurants there, and spent the past year cooking in my uncle's Italian restaurant in Twin Falls while taking business courses. It's been my dream since I was a teen to run my own kitchen."

Impressive. Dan had sold used cars until this opportunity with his dad had come up. He'd lacked the younger man's drive. Still lacked it.

"My original goal was to launch before I was thirty, but I

wasn't counting on my family's push to make it happen sooner. Two of my uncles here in Spokane are in construction, and Uncle Franco came across the perfect property on this side of downtown. Needs a load of renovation, but it will do nicely."

Must be nice to have a family that got behind a guy. Believed in him. Dad had put all his hopes into Dave Junior with nothing left over for his other two children.

"Anyway, I'm here to oversee renos and plan my restaurant's launch sometime next spring." Tony shook his head, grinning a little. "Hard to believe, but that's where I'm at. I'll also need a place to live. I'd thought of bunking with Alex, but his place is full up right now. As Nonna told you, no doubt, my aunts figure I should live with Nonna and look out for her."

Dan scratched his neck. "Yeah, that's what she told me. Said she didn't want someone underfoot."

"She doesn't seem to need supervision."

"Agreed. Not that I know her well. She's my landlady and the grandmother of some of my friends. I'm sure she's slowing down some as she ages, but I don't remember hearing anything about a health crisis."

"I'm sure she'd put me up, or I know Uncle Ray and Aunt Grace have room, but I wouldn't mind being useful as well as taking up space. I can set my own hours easily enough right now, since my uncles are doing the heavy lifting at the property. My main job seems to be making decisions."

"I can move Mandy in with her brothers for the time being, and I'll move into her room. You can have the master. I'll pay you—"

"I can't take your bedroom. The smaller one's fine, really. As for paying me, what's room and board worth around here these days?"

"I don't know."

Tony held up a hand. "I get that, if this works out, I'm meeting a need for your family. But, at the same time, you're meeting a need for me. I wasn't planning on mooching off of my nonna, either. I've been saving up for interim expenses."

Yes, Dan had been praying about the situation, but this? This was beyond his expectations. Well beyond. "I can't—"

"You'd be doing me a favor. Nonna rules her kitchen and will only let someone else in there begrudgingly. She'll let me cook for her sometimes if I ask nicely, but not all the time. I'm hoping you'd let me have some rein."

Were those tears pricking Dan's eyes? Since when did he get all emotional? Since Dixie had been giving him the runaround. "You want to cook for me? For the kids? And that's another thing. What do you know about children? Henry isn't potty-trained, and Buddy has an occasional accident still."

"My sister has two kids, a five-year-old son and a two-year-old daughter. I've watched them for the weekend a few times, and we all survived. I like kids, but I think I chose the wrong profession for a family of my own. Chefs' hours are wicked."

"I bet." Dan's mind still reeled. Could this really be the answer? "Want to give it, say, a week? If it doesn't work out for you, no worries. We can just part ways, and it will all be fine." Other than he'd still need a sitter.

"A week sounds like a fair trial. I've got a question, though."

"Oh?"

"What about the kids' mother? What will she think if I'm living here, watching her children?"

"I've spent three years wondering what Dixie will think of everything. I can't do it anymore." Dan grimaced, shaking his head. "My best suggestion is to use the dead-bolt, and don't let anyone in that you don't personally know. I'll introduce you to the neighbors."

"And your family?"

As if. "They're not in the picture."

Tony studied him a moment longer then nodded. "Tomorrow, then?"

11

*D*ixie squinted at the time as she reached for the phone. Ugh. Only eight-thirty, and she hadn't crawled back onto Tanisha's sofa until after four. And the caller was her mother. Ignoring Eunice Wayling was of no use. She'd just keep calling every two minutes until Dixie picked up.

She groaned and slumped back onto the rigid, threadbare arm. The phone went silent. Then a little beep signaled a voicemail. Dixie's headache pulsed, and her mouth felt like it had been stuffed full of cotton balls.

What had she been thinking, leaving Kristoff's at closing with those guys and moving on to the bar down the block? When the dancing part of the mobile party was over, she'd asked the bartender to call her a cab. The guys' interest in her was past borderline by then, and she wasn't too drunk to know she'd had enough. Enough beer. Enough groping.

She didn't want anyone but Dan, and he was too goody-two-shoes, like he hadn't slept around as much as she had.

As far as she knew, though, once he'd moved in with her, he'd been faithful.

Now he wanted to marry her, or at least he had last week. She'd likely burned that bridge along with every other on Thanksgiving Day.

Dixie forced herself upright and into the bathroom to take care of business. Brushing her teeth and gulping a glass of water also helped. Now for coffee... she might hate the stuff, but it did help with the inevitable.

Her phone rang. She took a deep breath and reached for it. "Hi, Mom."

"Dixie Dawn! Where are you?"

She winced. *Hello to you, too.* "Staying with Tanisha for a bit. Did you have a nice cruise?"

"Tanisha? Better than Dan Ranta, that..." She growled the string of obscenities she reserved for him, words he didn't deserve. Never had.

Dixie rubbed the center of her forehead. "Mom, stop. I asked you a question. How was the cruise?"

"Okay, I guess. You've been to one Caribbean island, you've seen them all."

How would Dixie know? She was pretty sure it wasn't true, but apparently Mom now wanted to play the blasé world traveler.

"Why did you go to Tanisha's? When I saw your stuff gone, I thought for sure you'd moved back in with Dan."

"It's a long story, but Dan and I are done."

"Finally. But where are the kids?"

Here it came. "With him."

"All three? Even Mandy?"

Dixie cringed at the shriek in Mom's voice. "Yeah.

They're better off with Dan than me." Because she was now working a night job and drinking too much. Again.

"You know he'll just dump them off at CPS when he gets tired of them. He probably already has."

Child Protection Services? Not Dan. He loved those kids. All of them. "He won't."

"I wouldn't count on it. Geez, Dixie, can't you do anything right?"

The familiar refrain bounced dully off her aching head. "No. I'm a loser like you've always said." *Just living up to expectations, Mom.*

Her mother sighed heavily into the phone. "So, Tanisha. How long is that going to last? You can't mooch off your friends forever like you did me."

"I'm not sure, but I'm not mooching. I've got a job."

"A job?"

Dixie could about see her mother's plucked eyebrows peak in disbelief. "Yeah, I'm working at K—" Did she *want* her mother showing up where she worked? Not at all. "At a bar on the east side."

"Good tips?"

They'd be better if Dixie flirted more. She tried, but Dan's brooding blue eyes accused her every time. "Not bad."

Mom huffed. "You tell Dan not to bother calling *me* if those kids are too much for him. He made his choice. He can deal with it."

Dixie'd had enough. "I'll tell him. Gotta go now." She clicked the phone off and stared out the window into the early December sky, thick with gray clouds.

Why had her mother always hated Dan so much? And,

by the sounds of it, she'd rather the kids, especially the boys, did go into foster care than sully her hands with them. She wasn't the cozy grandmotherly type, that was for sure. Each of the three was evidence of Dixie's screw-ups.

They were far more than the sum of their conceptions, though. Mandy idolized her mom so much, like Dixie had idolized hers. And just like Eunice Wayling had let Dixie down a thousand times, Dixie had done the same to her beautiful, delightful daughter. The little girl's devastated sobbing had wrenched her heart the other day. Still haunted her nightmares.

Buddy. Slow to speech... slow to hit most of his milestones, really. The little guy did everything with ferocity. He ran full tilt into everything, good or bad. Wasn't that just like his mama? Buddy adored Dan, and there couldn't be a better masculine role model for him.

And Dixie's sweet baby, Henry. He'd had his daddy since birth, unlike the others. He probably didn't even miss his mama. Why should he? She'd been an erratic presence at best in his young life.

Mom was right. Dixie was a loser. Her greatest failures — according to her mother, at least — were also her greatest blessings, but she was too messed up to do them justice. At least removing herself from their life also removed their toxic grandmother.

Dan would take good care of them. Maybe someday he'd meet a nice woman who'd... what, take on Dixie's mess? Yeah, not likely.

And if he did, Dixie'd forget to be grateful. She'd head right on over and scratch the woman's eyes out. Really? But she didn't want Dan for herself?

She did. She wanted him more than she could process. But not on his terms. On hers.

∽⊷⊱

DAN ENTERED Bridgeview Bakery and Bistro on Wednesday morning, Jacob and Tony on his heels.

"Good morning, guys. And you must be Tony Santoro." Wearing a friendly smile, Hailey came around the end of the counter and crossed the tile floor, hand outstretched. "I'm Hailey North. My cousin and I own this café, but I hear you're going to give us a run for our money."

Tony shook her hand. "I don't see any competition between an Italian restaurant and a chic bistro like yours."

Had the guy seriously just used the word *chic*?

Hailey fluttered her eyelashes. "I'm sure you're right. We close at five, after all."

"And Antonio's will open at four. Your cousin is Kassidy, right? She and I went to school together in Galena Landing."

"Yes. You missed your chance with her, though. She got married a few months ago and is already expecting their first child."

Tony smiled. "I'm happy for her. I'll be too busy with the new restaurant to date for quite a while. I'm sure you know what it's like."

Dan bit back the snort. Hailey might be a good businesswoman, but he'd hazard a guess she'd toss it all aside if a half-decent man offered the time of day. She certainly gave off that vibe, even to Dan, and he'd been firmly attached to Dixie the whole time he'd known Hailey.

Still was, but Dixie wasn't attached back.

A buzzer sounded from the kitchen, and Hailey waved toward the far end of the bistro where several men had already gathered around a series of pulled-together tables. "Your breakfast will be right out."

The guys greeted each other as Dan and Tony slid into their seats. The server, Shay, poured coffee all around then Hailey brought out a trolley loaded with hot breakfast sandwiches and fruit cups.

Peter offered grace before everyone dug in. "I just wanted to bring a word this morning before prayer time," he said. "I've been reading in the minor prophets lately. Have you really looked at Joel chapter two?"

Dan couldn't say that he had. He was still on perpetual repeat of the gospels, rereading the life of Jesus.

"This is the Lord talking to the people of Israel." Peter tapped on his screen, "Here's what He says: 'I will restore to you the years that the swarming locust has eaten, the hopper, the destroyer, and the cutter, my great army, which I sent among you. You shall eat in plenty and be satisfied, and praise the name of the Lord your God, who has dealt wondrously with you. And my people shall never again be put to shame. You shall know that I am in the midst of Israel, and that I am the Lord your God and there is none else. And my people shall never again be put to shame.'"

"Must be important," put in Jacob. "I notice God says it twice. 'My people shall never again be put to shame.'"

Across the table, Wesley Ferguson leaned on his elbows. "I like that bit about restoring the lost years. I really feel like that's been true in my life." His gaze found Tony's. "Don't know you, man, but let's just say my life took a wild ride before God reeled me in. I didn't even know He was fishing for me all that time."

Dan chuckled. "I hear you on that." He turned back to Peter. "Read that first part again?"

"Sure. 'I will restore to you the years that the swarming locust has eaten, the hopper, the destroyer, and the cutter, my great army, which I sent among you. You shall eat in plenty and be satisfied, and praise the name of the Lord your God, who has dealt wondrously with you.'" Peter looked up. "The locust and that other stuff represents our destructive behavior, all the junk that ruins our lives until God gets hold of us."

Never be put to shame. Wasn't that amazing? If only Dixie could hear that. Hear it and truly grasp it. Not that Dan understood all the nuances himself, but every day he spent in the Word, he latched onto a little more.

Peter set down his phone, had another bite of his egg sandwich, and swallowed. "Anyway, just wanted to share those verses about restoration. I read them over and over yesterday when I came across them and found great comfort."

Compared to Dan, Peter had lived an exemplary life. It was hard to imagine what he needed restoring from. Maybe the level of sin didn't matter so much. Everyone had done wrong, after all. Dan had realized that to the core of his soul. He'd needed redemption, but restoration was more. It wasn't just saving *from* something, but restoring *to* something even better. It put the positive spin to it.

"Reminds me of something in the psalms," Nathan Hamelin put in. "I think it's the second part of Psalm thirty, verse five."

Peter swiped his phone on and found it. "'Weeping may tarry for the night, but joy comes with the morning.'"

"That's the one. Do you have The Passion Translation in there? Because that was cool."

"Sure. Give me a second. 'We may weep through the night, but at daybreak it will turn into shouts of ecstatic joy.'"

"Yeah." Nathan pumped his fist lightly. "Like some of the rest of you, I went my way, too. Did a lot of things I'm not so proud of. But God forgave me when I repented. I'm not ashamed to admit there was weeping in the night as I came to my senses. But shouts of ecstatic joy at dawn? Yeah. I've had those, too. God is so faithful to restore. Some days I still marvel at it."

Shouts of joy in the morning? Dan felt like he was stuck in the crying-all-night stage, but it was nice to know there'd be a party at daybreak. If only Dixie'd be there to dance with him.

He cleared his throat. "Please keep praying for Dix."

Solemn eyes met his as his friends nodded. "You've got it, man. We're storming heaven's gates for her soul."

"Thanks."

12

*D*ixie shut the door on the courier and stared at the formidable envelope with an official-looking return address in the upper left corner. Dawson and Banks Family Law.

Her gut churned. Did she even want to read this? But she might as well, since she'd had to sign for the thing. Dawson and Banks had evidence she'd received it. With trembling fingers, she slit the envelope and pulled out a thick folded paper. Her gaze floated to the bottom. It was from Ms. S. Guthrie, Attorney at Law, Dawson and Banks Family Law.

The other shoe had dropped. Great.

Dear Ms. Wayling,

My client, Mr. Daniel John Ranta, has applied to the State of Washington for permanent custody of minor children Amanda Dawn Wayling, Buddy Carson Wayling, and Henry Donovan Wayling.

Mr. Ranta claims...

The words blurred, and the room swam around Dixie.

How could Dan do this to her? Oh, she knew. Of course, she knew. Everyone had a limit, and she'd reached Dan's. Wasn't this what she wanted? The kids were better off without her. She'd come to that conclusion many times and stuck by her decision for over a week now. She'd burned all her bridges when she'd locked a crying child alone in that house.

This was it, then. If she didn't fight this stupid letter, she'd never see her children again. Mandy's brown eyes implored her mama not to leave. Buddy angled his curly head up at her with a skeptical side-eye. The baby reached dimply arms toward her, his adorable grin threatening to melt all the ice in her soul.

What had she been thinking, walking away from her children? How could she know if they really were better off without her? Her head was so muddled, and it wasn't all booze. Drinking and dancing and partying weren't as much fun as they used to be when she and Dan were together. Drat him, anyway.

Or not. The guy was a rock. She needed him to be a rock as much as she hated him for it.

Dixie rubbed her forehead, where a band of tension cinched ever tighter. Leaving was supposed to make things easier. Easier and more stable for the kids. Easier for Dan — except for the whole childcare thing — and definitely easier for her.

If this were easier, she couldn't take harder. Kristoff was after her to tease more at the bar. Apparently, men complained she was standoffish. Yeah, well, they weren't Dan, okay? She didn't want to hop into bed with just any old guy. Dan had spoiled her.

Dan loved her. Wanted to marry her, to form a family. What was she running from?

Without finishing the letter — she could imagine the rest of it just fine, thanks — she flipped her phone to the prodigal son story Linnea had talked about.

Dan had once installed The Passion Translation app on her cell. She'd mocked the name but hadn't bothered to delete it. She didn't need to read the entire sordid tale of the young man again. Just the good parts.

From a long distance away, his father saw him coming, dressed as a beggar, and great compassion swelled up in his heart for his son who was returning home. So the father raced out to meet him. He swept him up in his arms, hugged him dearly, and kissed him over and over with tender love.

Dixie scrubbed her eyes. What would it be like to be so treasured? If she'd ever seen that kind of love, her life would never have taken the road it had. But hadn't this guy's father ever shown him love before he left? He must've, or the guy wouldn't have had the nerve to return.

Then the son said, 'Father, I was wrong. I have sinned against you. I could never deserve to be called your son. Just let me be—'

The father interrupted and said, 'Son, you're home now!'

What if it wasn't Dan and the kids she'd run away from? What if it really was God? She'd made sure to stay away from any whales, just in case, but she'd made a joke about it. God probably had more ways than giant marine mammals to get someone's attention.

For the guy in this story, it was pig slop. Ugh.

Turning to his servants, the father said, 'Quick, bring me the best robe, my very own robe, and I will place it on his shoulders.

Bring the ring, the seal of sonship, and I will put it on his finger. And bring out the best shoes you can find for my son.'

The father hadn't held anything back, had he? That ungrateful son who'd stormed off and made a total mess of his life — much like she had — was fully restored. Dixie didn't have to understand the robe and shoes bit to get the gist.

Now that was love. Her eyes skimmed to the next few verses.

Let's prepare a great feast and celebrate. For this beloved son of mine was once dead, but now he's alive again. Once he was lost, but now he is found! And everyone celebrated with overflowing joy.

It was just a wonderful, hopeful story, right? Linnea had even said so, that it was a story Jesus told. It hadn't even happened, like ever. It was only to make a point.

Dixie thumbed through the next few chapters, skimming bits here and there. Seemed like Jesus really liked to tell stories. There were a lot of them. Her eyes caught on a few words: *The Son of Man has come to seek out and to give life to those who are lost.*

Son of Man? A quick search showed that to be another name for Jesus. The sentence matched up to what Dan said, that Jesus' mission had been to bring life to those who needed it.

She might've laughed in Dan's face, but that didn't mean she hadn't heard the words. Apparently, at least some of them had stuck.

Great. She'd cut off the one person who could answer questions about Jesus. There were others. Linnea, but she was little improvement over Dan. Fran Amato. Other Bridgeview residents, but Dixie had mostly kept her distance from the whacko religious bunch. They were all wrapped up in Dan, anyway.

Not that she wanted to hear more about Jesus. She closed the Bible app, set the phone down, and picked up the letter again.

Words like *non-parent custody* and *no visitation* and *challenge this petition* jumped out at her. This whole missive was full of legal jargon. She didn't dare agree with anything unless she understood what it meant. It seemed obvious enough on the surface — Dan was booting her out of the kids' lives and claiming full custody — but what if she missed a loophole?

What if she straightened up her life in a year or two and wanted to see the kids again? If she went along with this, was it forever? And... she stared at the far wall until it blurred. If she contemplated straightening up her life later, why not now?

A noise behind her caused her to whirl, but it was only Tanisha emerging from her bedroom. Her friend's gaze toggled between Dixie's face and the letter in her hand. "Thought I heard the door buzzer."

"You did." Dixie held up the paper. "Dan's filing for custody."

"Oh, hon." Tanisha grimaced. "Don't let him get away with that. I mean, he's a decent guy and all, but the kids need you."

Dixie stiffened. Not this again. "I need someone to talk to about what it all means down the road."

"I don't know anyone legal."

"Yeah, me neither. Except Dan's brother, and that's no help." Dixie looked back at the paper with its sprawling signature above the words *Ms. S. Guthrie, Attorney at Law.* "I could maybe call this office and get some info."

Tanisha laughed. "It'll cost you."

Dixie didn't have that much money, not with keeping her car going and paying Tanisha for her share of the rent. No way Mom would help. Nobody would. She didn't have anyone waiting for her to wise up like the prodigal son did.

THE SNOW HAD HELD OFF, so far, and Tony had been willing for Dan to get a head start on implementing a design proposal for a new client. Tony said he could work on menu plans on his laptop as well at the house as anywhere for a few days. Dan was going to owe his new friend big-time.

"Smells great in here." Dan left his boots on the mat and hung his jacket before coming through to the main living area. Walking into the aroma of yeasty bread and garlic-and-tomato-laden sauce was definitely something he could get used to at the end of a long day.

"Daddy's home!" yelled Buddy, scooting down the stairs bump, bump, bump on his backside. "Hi, Daddy!"

"Mama said he's not your daddy." Mandy parked her hands on her hips and glared at her brother.

"Is so." Buddy squeezed all the circulation out of Dan's thigh. "Right, Daddy?"

"Close enough." Dan scooped Buddy into his arms and pulled Mandy against his side. "Hey, Mandy-girl. How was school today?"

She leaned in. "Okay. We had dance after at the church.

How come Tieri's mama goes to practice with her and mine doesn't?"

Some questions had no answers. "I'm sorry, baby." He rubbed her shoulder. "Do you want to show me what you practiced?"

She shook her head and pulled away before preceding him into the kitchen, where Henry sat on the floor, gnawing a crust of bread. The little guy clambered to his feet and toddled over for his own greeting. Dan hugged him, looking at Tony over his son's head. "How was today?"

"Good." The other man grinned and patted Mandy's hair.

"Mr. Tony can make real bread, and he isn't even a store!" Mandy's eyes shone in admiration as she looked up at their houseguest. "And it's so yummy and warm and the butter even melts on it. You should have some."

Dan's stomach growled even as he chuckled at Mandy's awe. "Can't wait." As much as he longed for Dixie, having Tony living in was a true gift from God. Not only for the early mornings still to come, but the food! Dan was going to gain fifty pounds this winter.

"Dinner's ready." Tony turned off a burner. "Now, Mandy, I want your honest opinion, okay? I want to know if this dinner is the kind kids will want to order at my restaurant."

At least Mandy was pleased with *Tony's* attention. "Yes, Mr. Tony. I'm sure they will. It smells so yummy."

"And you need to try it both ways, with noodles and zoodles. I need your advice."

"What's zoodles?"

"A different kind of noodles, a kind made from veggies."

Mandy frowned but nodded. "I'll tell you what I think."

Dan herded the boys into the main floor bath for hand-washing then back to the table. He lifted Henry into his high chair as Tony set bowls on the table. Biting her lip in concentration, Mandy carried a plate stacked with garlic toast.

Man, he was hungry. Dan issued a short prayer of thanks then scooped a meatball and some of the zucchini noodles onto Henry's tray before dishing up for the older boy.

"Why do you make noodles out of veggies?" Mandy asked Tony.

"There are a couple of reasons." Tony ladled food for her. "One, everybody needs more vegetables, because they help kids and grownups be strong and healthy. And also, because sometimes people eat so much other stuff that they don't have room for veggies or other things that are super good for them."

"Don' like veggies," announced Buddy, jamming his fork into the sauce-covered zoodles.

Dan wasn't about to break it to him. He scooped pasta onto his plate then hesitated before adding the zoodles on top and giving the combo a twirl. Then he piled on sauce and meatballs. He could be a good example for the kids. It was enough that somebody else was cooking.

And, hey, the combo didn't taste half bad.

"This is yummy, Mr. Tony." Mandy set her fork down. "Kids up to age ten will like this food."

Dan stifled a chuckle at her serious tone.

Tony nodded at the little girl. "Not eleven-year-olds, though? What should I cook for them?"

"Maybe macaroni and cheese instead. Or a different noodle."

"I'll keep that in mind."

"I think you should, Mr. Tony."

Dan stared out the patio door, struggling not to laugh out loud.

Mandy had been supremely annoyed about moving into her brothers' bedroom to open space for Tony, but it hadn't taken the newcomer long to win her over. Next thing Dan knew, she'd be taking all the credit for the kids' menu at Antonio's when it opened in spring.

"Want more." Buddy pushed his bowl at Dan. "Please."

"Sure thing."

The kid hadn't even clued in he'd been eating zucchini. Wouldn't Dixie be shocked to see her kids inhaling vegetables?

Dan's heart squeezed. Had she received the papers yet? Sadie had promised to keep him up-to-date, but the wait was killing him.

Was he really doing the right thing?

13

*D*ixie tugged her skirt straight, took a deep breath, and tapped the elevator button in the posh lobby downtown. Dawson and Banks Family Law inhabited the offices on the eleventh floor. She clutched her bright red handbag as she rode up.

The doors opened onto a glass and chrome reception room, and an elegant woman glanced up from behind the desk. Her blond hair was pulled into a formal updo above a flawless face. She pushed rhinestone-studded glasses up, as her mouth, rimmed with matte lipstick in a coral tone so deep it neared copper, opened to speak.

Dixie stared. She figured she was on-trend, but more money kicked fashion up a notch. She felt like a tramp pretending to be someone greater.

Because she was.

The elevator doors began to swish shut, but Dixie pressed her hand against the edge to stop them, her gaze never leaving the receptionist.

This was a mistake — a horrible mistake — but she was

used to making those, and she was here now. That woman had been staring at her long enough to pick her out of a police lineup, so she might as well state her case and flee. If Dan could afford this firm, Dixie didn't stand a chance. She didn't, anyway, so what did it matter?

The automatic doors made another effort to close.

Dixie took a deep breath and strode toward the desk, her thigh-high boots clicking on the marble floor.

The woman rose at her approach, and a smile softened her face. "May I help you?"

Dixie glanced at the name — Ms. H. Simmons — etched on the chrome nameplate. "Hi, I'm Dixie Wayling, and I'd like to speak with Ms. Guthrie."

"Do you have an appointment?"

"Um, no, but I just need a minute." Any bravado Dixie had managed to muster was long gone.

"I'm sorry, but Ms. Guthrie is fully booked today; neither is she taking on new clients at this time."

Dixie shifted the straps of her red purse on her shoulder. "Okay. I'm sure I can't afford her, anyway. This was a mistake." She backed up two steps. "I'm sorry for wasting your time."

"Ms. Wayling, the State of Washington has resources for anyone who needs a lawyer but cannot afford one." Ms. Simmons plucked a pamphlet out of a rack on her desk. "Give this number a call and see what they can do."

Dixie stared at the paper. "It probably won't make a difference. I blew any chance I had already, and my ex is filing for custody of the kids." She blinked back a tear. "With the help of Ms. Guthrie."

"Ms. Wayling."

She looked up. Wait, was the older woman actually showing sympathy? More likely she was shocked by how pathetic Dixie was.

"Perhaps you might seek counseling?" Ms. Simmons still held the leaflet out. "Washington Law Help may be able to assist you with personal counsel as well as legal."

Dixie huffed a sigh, ending on a near sob. "I don't know. It's probably too late. I don't know what to do."

"Try. You'll never know if you don't try."

Wasn't that the truth? Dixie took the pamphlet, if only so the receptionist wouldn't feel obligated to extend it forever. She tried for a smile. "Thanks."

"You're very welcome, Ms. Wayling."

Ms. Simmons probably knew all about the letter. She'd probably written it, held it out for the lawyer to sign, then sealed it and ordered the courier.

Dixie searched the older woman's eyes. The gaze was steady. Sympathetic. Dixie nodded and broke the connection as she turned away. It took a minute for the elevator car to arrive, but Dixie didn't look back. She managed to press the lobby button without making eye contact with the receptionist again. When the doors finally closed, she sagged against the wall and closed her eyes.

What a mess she'd made. She could blame her mom all she wanted, but she'd made her own choices. She couldn't blame Brandon or Scott or Dan, either. Dan least of all. Sure, he'd grown up in a two-parent household, but his home life had been a mess just the same. He'd earned an honest living selling used cars then stepped back into the family business without holding a grudge against his bully of a father. Dixie had made her choices. So had Dan, but he'd faced his like an adult, where Dixie had hugged her selfishness tighter as she ran.

She exited the building and sat on a bench outside. What were her options? If she even had any.

The kids needed Dan. He'd be their anchor, be a better parent than Dave Senior or Yvonne or Dixie's mom. Better than Dixie, for sure. But Tanisha's and Billie's words wouldn't leave her mind. They both agreed how messed up their mothers' rejections had made them.

Could she do that to Mandy and Buddy and Henry?

She already had.

But was it permanent? The official letter full of legalese sounded like it. If that thing went through, it would all be over.

Dixie fingered the pamphlet the receptionist had given her. If she started working with these people, she had to change. She couldn't keep being Dixie Wayling, the woman who refused responsibility, rejected rescue, and ran from her problems.

How did a person do that, anyway? Just up and decide to be someone different?

God doesn't care about your past. Dan's earnest face materialized in her mind. *He's ready to forgive you and welcome you into His family. He did it for me, and He wants to do it for you. You just have to ask.*

That sounded all too simplistic, really. Why would God wave His magic wand for her? What had she ever done for Him? Nothing. Dan had been a good guy before he found Jesus. No wonder Jesus welcomed him in. So, Dixie needed to figure out how to be a good person. A worthy person. Someone God could forgive and smile kindly on, like the father of the prodigal son. They'd already been related before the story started, so of course the father would be happy to see him.

Just like Dixie would always love her own kids, no matter what they did, just because they were her kids. Even if she had to leave them to give them a better life... but was she actually accomplishing that?

She rubbed her temples. The panicking thoughts swirled in ever-deepening spirals. She needed an off-ramp in the worst way, and she needed it *now* if she were to make the best possible decision for the kids. Should she just let Dan claim them? Or should she fight back?

Calling the number on the pamphlet was a good first step. At least, she'd be able to see what her options were.

If she had any left.

PETER WANDERED into the kitchen to taste-test Tony's latest creation while Sadie settled into the armchair across from Dan.

"Has there been any word?" Dan hated that he couldn't keep the pleading out of his voice, but this mess with Dixie was tearing him apart.

"Not officially." Sadie studied him. "She has one week to respond. That's what I stated in the letter, which was delivered at three-twelve yesterday afternoon according to the courier stamp."

A week. He was going to be stark raving mad in seven days. This whole thing was such a wreck. He didn't want to parent without Dixie. He wanted her at his side as his wife, his partner in every way. But she resisted at every turn, and he'd been forced into a corner.

"Unofficially, however..."

His gaze riveted back on Sadie's, hope bubbling. "Yes?"

"She came by the office today and talked to Hazel at the reception desk."

Dan waited.

"I'll admit to eavesdropping from just inside my office. She sounded... Dan, I hate to ask, but do you think she'd do anything drastic?"

"Drastic?" His mind swung to Sadie's meaning. *No.*

"She sounded so bleak when she said it was all too late, it was all I could do not to run out there. Maybe I should have, but Hazel seemed to be handling her fine, offering her resources. I couldn't have done much else, not in a professional capacity."

Dan shook his head. "Her mood swings can get pretty volatile, but I've never considered her suicidal. I'm no expert, though."

"Are you keeping in touch with her?"

"I text her every day. Tell her something the kids have done." He scrubbed a hand across his eyes. "Maybe I shouldn't be doing that. As my legal counsel, should I stop?"

"I'm not going to insist, but do think about whether you're giving her tools she could use against you. She knows Mandy is at the church after school on Tuesdays, for instance. Might she show up there?"

"Fran wouldn't let Dixie take her. She knows enough of what's going on, as she's still involved in the boys' care."

"Right, and Dixie knows that, too. My concern is that

she knows too much of how to get to the children. To get you where it hurts."

"She wouldn't." Would she? He couldn't think it of her. But then, she'd taken Mandy at Thanksgiving, even if she'd thought better of it within minutes.

"Don't let love blind you, Dan."

He pulled to his feet and paced to the window, where soft, gentle snowflakes were floating. He'd have to check throughout the night to determine if enough accumulated to warrant getting the Bobcats out. But first, Sadie.

Dan turned back to his friend. "I don't know what else to do. My sister's been in touch with Dixie, too. They spoke once, but Dixie's blocked Linnea's calls ever since. She's back in the bar scene, back to working nights at Kristoff's, back with our old friends. That's how I found where she's at, through Jared and Billie. Jared was sympathetic, but what can he do? And none of them are believers. Their advice to her is based on their experience outside of faith."

"Letting go is so hard."

"You're telling me."

The two cousins' deep laughter erupted from the kitchen as the aroma of something like doughnuts and honey swirled toward him. Tony had mentioned making struffoli tonight. The guy was a godsend. Dan should be taking a cooking lesson or two while he had a master chef living in his house.

Sadie grimaced as she glanced toward the kitchen. Right, she was on some kind of sugar-free diet. That didn't bode well for whatever Tony and Peter were cooking up at the moment. "So," she said. "If I hear anything before next Tuesday, I'll let you know."

"That's all I can ask. We need to watch out for Eunice — Dixie's mom — too. A woman matching her description came by the house today, but Tony didn't open the door. I don't know what she wants with me or the kids. She's made no secret she despises me and thinks the kids are a drag on Dixie's life. I'd think she'd be happy with the current situation."

"As happy as a bitter woman like her can be?"

"I guess. The school knows not to let anyone but Fran or me pick up Mandy. She used to walk home with Violet Sheridan, but I can't risk that right now. I don't know if you know Violet, but she made a bit of a stink. She's only nine — definitely not big enough to protect Mandy, but I didn't want to explain why. I told the kids it was because of the colder weather, and Violet said it wasn't *that* cold." Dan shook his head. "She's right, of course."

Sadie chuckled. "Reason doesn't work on Violet, anyway. She's quite the kid."

"Seems like. Oh, and Rebekah Roper is meeting with Mandy at Bridgeview Elementary, too. She's the school counselor."

"And your neighbor," pointed out Sadie.

"Right. But we're doing this by the book."

"Except for you texting Dixie."

He spread his hands. "Am I supposed to cut off all contact?"

Sadie met his gaze. "It might be best. If you're asking for my official advice, that would be my suggestion."

Dan turned back to the window. Could he really give up all communication with Dixie? She rarely texted him back. When she did, it was a simple answer like *cool* or *nice*.

Nothing to say how she felt or what she was doing or if she missed him or the kids.

Lord, what do I do?

It wasn't the first time he'd asked. But maybe it was the first time he didn't assume he knew best. Handing his hopes, his dreams, his desires over to the Lord and leaving them there would be the hardest thing he'd ever done.

Was God asking him to cut Dixie off, or was that just Sadie Guthrie, Attorney at Law, speaking?

14

*D*ixie hadn't stepped foot in Bridgeview for three weeks, and never in the doors of the white clapboard church. She studied the building from the safety of her car. There'd been enough snow overnight that someone had plowed the parking area and shoveled the sidewalks. Dan, maybe? She had no idea if he had this contract. A year ago, there was no way he'd have submitted a bid to a church. So much had changed.

Like Dixie entering a house of worship. Desperate times called for desperate measures, though. When she'd seen the name Juanita Ramirez in the list of available counselors, it had sounded familiar enough for her to check it out. Seemed the woman was, indeed, the pastor's wife that Dan had talked about.

Maybe she should rethink. Maybe it would be a better idea to bare her soul to someone with no preconceived opinions about her tangled mess. On the other side, it was a shortcut, and a pastor's wife should be able to tell her how to become good enough for Dan and for God. She kept reading that story over and over until she wanted that kind of end result for herself. *And everyone celebrated with over-flowing joy.*

Of course, it might not be possible. She might not have run off with her inheritance — as if there'd be anything when her mom kicked the bucket — or eaten pig swill, but she still felt for the guy where it talked about his *binge of extravagant and reckless living.*

Been there, done that, got the T-shirt.

Dixie shoved her car door open and stepped into the cold December wind. She tugged her jacket tighter, grabbed her purse, and headed to the side door. Inside the building, warmth greeted her in a small lobby. A carved nativity scene sat on a golden tablecloth, surrounded by pine cones and several squat pillar candles with flickering flames. The aromas of cinnamon and ginger mixed with the pine infiltrated the air, and orchestral Christmas music flowed from hidden speakers.

Christmas. It was just a week away. There was no Christmas tree in Dixie's life. No wrapped gifts, no iced cookies, no small faces lit with wonder. She swallowed hard.

"Dixie?" A small Latina woman stood in a doorway across the space. "I'm Juanita. Come on in. May I pour you some coffee or tea?"

"Tea would be nice. Thank you." Dixie followed Juanita into the welcoming room with two comfortable armchairs. A family portrait, surrounded by framed children's artwork adorned the walls. While Juanita fixed the tea, Dixie examined the photo. "You have a lovely family." Her voice choked on the words.

"God has blessed Tomas and me beyond measure,"

Juanita answered, setting two teacups on the round table between the armchairs. She moved to stand beside Dixie. "Sabrina is our eldest. She's nine. Then Emmanuel — Manny — who's seven. And our baby, Isaac, who's two." She angled a look toward Dixie. "You also have a girl and then two boys, right?"

Dixie nodded, tears blinding her. "You probably know them."

"I've seen them with Dan, yes. Your Mandy is a lovely little lady, a born dancer. I've popped in to watch the practices a few times, since my son is in the group, too. Mandy has natural grace."

"She... she's amazing. I guess that's why I'm here. I don't deserve to be her mother, but I want to be." Dixie gestured toward the family portrait. "You seem to have it together. Can you tell me how?"

"May I ask God's guidance in our talk today?"

"Okay."

It definitely wasn't peace that settled over Dixie as the woman prayed out loud. Instead, it might have been a yearning. All she knew was that it was going to get mighty uncomfortable before it got better. If it ever did.

DAN TAPPED on the door of his parents' house then entered. He set Henry down and unzipped the tyke's jacket while Buddy kicked off his boots.

"Daniel." Dad leaned against the arch that led to the living room.

"Hi, Dad." He turned to the boys. "Play nicely while I talk to Grandpa."

Buddy nodded. "Come, Henry. I share cars." Then he ran toward the basket in the living room with his little brother toddling behind him.

Dad's chin jerked toward the kitchen. "Pour yourself a coffee."

"Thanks. Will do." There'd been several three a.m. mornings in a row. Took a lot of caffeine to keep a guy going, even when he crashed asleep as soon as he'd tucked the kids in at night.

"How're things? The business?"

"Good. If the almanac is right and we get a lot of snow this winter, I'll be turning contracts away."

"Buy another Bobcat."

"Then I need another experienced operator, and I don't know anyone looking for work." Nor did he want the added debt when life was so uncertain.

"I could fill in some."

Dan chuckled and took a sip of his black coffee. "Mom told me not to let you."

Dad's chest puffed out. "She's not the boss of me. I'll work if I want to."

"I appreciate having you on standby in case someone calls in sick. I'd rather keep our current clients happy than add more."

"You need to think bigger."

"Running three is enough. We can keep them busy all summer, too. Another one would spend too much time idle."

Dad huffed.

Must be hard to give up the reins to something a man had built. Dan softened his voice. "With Linnea and Logan returning in April, we'll expand in landscape design. More money. Less risk."

"They won't be repeat customers. Design a yard, and it's over. Especially the way your sister is talking with natural grasses and such. Where's the maintenance contracts with that?"

"There'll be plenty. I get emails and calls every week looking for more information on our new greener policies."

Dad snorted. "Every week? Big whoopedy-do. You know most of those won't come through. Phone calls don't amount to a hill of beans."

"Good thing," Dan said mildly. "Or I'd need to be ten guys. But it's early winter, coming on Christmas, and folks are busy with other things. It'll pick up in the new year. You'll see."

"I doubt it. You'll run Ranta Landscaping into the ground with your lofty ideals."

"Haven't managed that yet in two years. Not too worried about it happening now." Dan leaned against the kitchen cupboard and took another sip of coffee. "You and Mom given any thought to coming to the program at the church Sunday night? Mandy's doing real well with her dancing."

"She's not even your kid."

"I've filed for full custody."

"You what? You're a dang-blamed fool, taking on that b—"

"Shush, Dad. Don't let the boys hear you talking about their mother that way."

His father cast a glance toward the living room. "You know what I'm talking about."

Yeah, he sure did. "Dixie's got through the weekend to contest the orders. I haven't heard from her in a few days, so I'm not sure what she's thinking."

Dad cursed under his breath.

"It's bad timing, right before Christmas, but my attorney said not to let things slide."

"Your attorney." Dad shook his head. "I hope you're not expecting the business to pay for that."

"Not at all. It's covered."

"I notice you didn't hire your brother."

"Dave Junior's in criminal defense. I needed someone working in family law."

His dad huffed again.

"I know you don't understand my choices, but I need you to try. I'm not abandoning Dixie. I'm trying to protect the kids, especially because of what happened at Thanksgiving."

"How many times do I have to tell you? They're not your responsibility."

"Henry's mine—"

"You sure?"

Dan rolled his eyes. "Have you even *looked* at him? He's the spitting image of my baby pictures. Mom even says so."

"You should get a paternity test done."

"No need. It changes nothing. And the other two are my son's siblings. I'm the only father they've ever known. Mandy was two when I met Dixie. There's no way I'm ditching them to the foster care system or spending my life worrying about whether Dixie's caring for them properly. They need stability. I'm it."

"Is this the kind of thing religion is filling your head with?"

"Being a responsible grownup? I think that's pretty basic. But a relationship with Jesus certainly helps keep me focused and grounded. Gives me hope."

"He's a dead guy, Daniel. You might as well tell me you've been hanging out with Napoleon."

"Then you might want to stop using God's name as a curse word. If it doesn't mean anything, anyway, what's the point?"

Dad blinked. "I hardly think—"

"That's the thing. Yeah, Jesus was born a long time ago. He lived. He died. But then He rose again, because He's God. If He hadn't risen, the world would be a much different place. It would be like evil darkness everywhere, all the time. He's the one who gives light, who gives the promise of a bright sunrise to come. I know it sounds like a fairy tale to you, but I promise if you open your mind and heart to it, even a little bit, you'll begin to see what I'm talking about. There's hope for a brighter tomorrow, Dad. Not only that, but there's a helping hand in getting through the long night."

"Logan teaching you to preach? I don't want to hear about your delusions."

"Come to the concert on Sunday? Linnea and Logan will be back from Edmonds. I know they wouldn't miss it for anything. You could sit with them in the back."

"Your mother wants to go, but I think I'll stay home. It's not like Mandy is—"

"Dad."

"Well, it's true. I don't know how you turned into this bleeding heart for someone else's offspring."

Dan leaned in and captured his father's gaze. "Unlike some people, I have the capacity to love more than one child at a time."

Dad's eyes narrowed. "What's that supposed to mean?"

"It means you've never given a whit about Linnea or me. You only seem capable of loving your namesake. Why? What did we do to deserve shunting to the side?"

Dad's mouth worked as though he was figuring out how to deny the accusation. Then he slumped against the counter. "You don't know what it was like."

"You're right. I don't. Because we all have the capacity to love infinitely."

"He was so sick. We nearly lost him over and over."

"Dave Junior?"

Dad nodded, averting his gaze. "Something with his breathing. I can't remember what they called it."

"So, you decided it wasn't worth loving your other kids? Because then you wouldn't have to be worried about them? Because that's sick." Hot rage flared.

"It wasn't like that." But the words carried no force.

Dan gripped his cup, trying to keep his mouth shut so he wouldn't say anything he'd have to apologize for. Talk about a battle. He poured the last of his coffee down the drain. "I have to leave now. Boys!" He elbowed past his dad.

"Daniel..."

Dan swooped Henry into his arms. "Come on, Buddy. Boots and jacket."

"But I play cars."

"You can play with your racetrack at home."

The little guy angled his head upward. "Play wif me?"

"Sure, I can do that for a little while." Dan raised his voice. "Because I love you."

Take that, Dad.

⌒ℓ⌐

"How do I get good enough for God?" Dixie couldn't hold the question back. It had been burning in her for several days now. "That prodigal son — his father gave a big party for him, but that's because they were related. I mean, I kind of get that part. I love my kids." Her voice choked. "But I'm nobody to God."

Juanita's brown eyes warmed. Compassion? Hopefully not pity. "You're everything to God."

"Yeah, don't mess with me. It's a serious question."

"And I'm giving you a serious answer. God wants nothing more than to welcome you into His family. He wants to heal you, make you whole, and give you hope and a future. It's the entire reason Jesus came to earth as a baby and grew up to die for you."

Dixie shook her head. "There are over seven billion people on the planet today, and that's not even counting how many people have lived and died since that happened. There's no way He cares about me."

"I understand what you're saying. It does seem like a wild claim."

She'd known it all along. Even so, she felt hope drip out through the parched cracks of her soul.

Juanita leaned closer. "But it's still true. We don't have

to become good enough for God to accept us. We never could. I mean, if it were possible, we wouldn't have needed Jesus to die for us, right? We could just be good enough by ourselves."

"I guess." It made sense, in a weird sort of way.

"Do you enjoy reading? I've got a book I'd love to give you that explains it much more clearly than I can in one or two sessions."

"I don't read much." Unless fashion magazines counted. "But I could try. The thing is, I don't have a lot of time. I have to appear in court the first week of January."

"Are you here only because of the custody case?"

Dixie shook her head. "No. Dan's definitely the better parent. I'm going to lose if it goes to court. I haven't done anything right, and I mostly haven't cared. But... that story haunts me. The prodigal son one. Did you know that 'everyone celebrated with overflowing joy'? I want to believe that could happen for me, and that it would make a difference."

Juanita covered Dixie's hand with her own. "It can. Let me make some calls and see if we can get that court appearance pushed back."

Hope flickered like the first rays of dawn after the blackest night. "You could do that? Get me time?"

"I can try."

15

"Have you heard from Dan lately?" Juanita welcomed Dixie into her office two days later.

Dixie shook her head. "Not since I went into Dawson and Banks. Probably his high-falutin' attorney advised against it. Or maybe he gave up talking to a brick wall." Now she regretted staying aloof. Not acting more interested. Even though she stifled motherly feelings didn't mean she didn't have any.

"It's probably just as well. Can I make you tea?"

Tea? Dixie blinked. "Um, sure."

She watched as the counselor poured two cups and set them on the round table. The other woman settled into her seat, took a long sip, and stared into the distance. Probably wondering what kind of loser Dixie was — a mother feigning indifference to her own kids. "I do love them, you know. The kids."

Juanita's deep brown eyes focused on Dixie. "Of course, you do."

"I mean, I know what it looks like."

"What do you think it looks like?"

Dixie considered her words. "There are two kinds of people in this world. Optimists and pessimists. Experience taught me it's best to have low expectations. You're not as likely to get hurt."

Yeah, right. Shards still slashed. Blood still poured. Pain still shattered.

"What was your home life like as a child?"

Dixie could almost hear the Freudian, *tell me about your mother*. "My father was a traveling salesman with a wife in Pasco and a girlfriend — my mother — in Spokane. My mom was livid when she found out about the other woman, because my father made her believe she was his one and only. Turned out he had other women along his route, too."

Juanita grimaced. "Sounds like a real winner."

"So, Mom refused to see him again, which was fine by him since the idea of an illegitimate baby was messing with his marriage. And my mother..." Dixie hesitated. "Well, she wasn't around much, either. She was busy with work, busy with men. She hung out at the bar a lot..."

Oh, man. Just what she'd always wanted: to become her mother. A sick sensation swarmed her stomach at the thought.

"Did she — does she — love you?"

"In her own way, I guess. More than if I'd been a boy." Dixie lifted a shaky hand to sip her tea, barely managing not to slosh the hot liquid. "See, if you give a kid hope, they'll run with it and expect good things."

"As a child, you expected better."

"Yeah." She really had, even though Mom hadn't given her much reason for it. Kids must be born optimists. Thoughts of Mandy's sparkling eyes, Buddy's throat-strangling hugs, and Henry's warm cheek on her shoulder demonstrated that. "My kids do, too," she whispered, taking a quick swipe below her eye to catch a drip.

Juanita laid a tissue in her lap.

"Thanks." Dixie worked to get her emotions under control. She really didn't need this counselor, this pastor's wife, thinking she was some fragile emotional crybaby. Not a chance. Dixie was strong. She was immune. She was...

Frail. Needy.

She sniffled again. She wouldn't cry. She just wouldn't.

"It's okay, Dixie. This is a safe place. Let it all out. You'll feel better for it."

She jerked her head from side to side. Dabbed her eyes. Swallowed hard. Folded her hands tightly in her lap. Squared her shoulders.

A weak weepy woman wouldn't regain rights to her kids. On the other hand, what did she have to lose? She'd already lost everything.

No bawling, Dix. You've got it coming.

"It's hard to overcome lack of love in childhood, I think." Juanita spoke softly. "To feel like nobody's got your back, and there's no safe place."

The woman had that right.

"Which makes it hard to parent your own children differently. You don't have the tools."

Dixie shot Juanita a sidelong look. The counselor had more tears in her eyes than Dixie did.

Chin up. "I bet you don't get it. Your life has probably been a bed of roses. You're a pastor's wife. You probably have a perfect marriage and perfect kids. It comes easy to people like you."

Juanita shook her head. "I was thinking of how my mom raised five kids alone, on almost no money, after my dad went to jail for theft."

No way.

"I was the oldest and had a lot of responsibility. I got the little kids up for school because Mom was asleep from her night job in a factory. Sometimes Mom made supper. More often, I did. It was a lot to put on an eleven-year-old."

"Really? And yet you turned into a decent human being." Unlike Dixie.

Juanita met her gaze. "It was God's grace. Nothing more. Nothing less. The church around the corner got wind of our situation and began to help out. One by one, they led our family to Jesus."

Like Bridgeview Bible Church was doing for Dan. According to Juanita, like they wanted to do for Dixie, too. Why did she resist? What would she gain by digging in her heels?

She felt like a little lost child, shivering with cold, peering into a scene all decorated for Christmas. Happy children inside danced with joy at the gifts under the tree with its twinkling lights. Smiling unknown grownups passed out hot cocoa with peppermint sticks and mounds of whipped cream. Flames crackled in a brick fireplace, and happy music played softly.

Everyone inside that perfect scene looked so content. It

was every child's dream. It had been Dixie's, but it hadn't been her reality. She'd rarely received what she wanted, and none of it had been given with love and joy. Mom made sure Dixie knew how stupid Christmas was, that Santa wasn't real no matter what her friends said, and that she should just be thankful for what she had.

Mom had seemed determined to squelch any optimism Dixie might muster. Maybe she thought she was protecting her daughter, inoculating her against future disappointments. It hadn't worked. Pain still sabotaged her at every turn.

Why then did she think withholding love would work on her own kids? But it wasn't even that. Deep inside, clarity exploded. She pushed her kids away, not to help them understand the difficulties of life from an early age, but to protect *herself* from the day they'd inevitably move on from their mother.

How sick was that?

Dixie clutched her arms around her belly and rocked in her chair. It wasn't for her kids' sake. It was for her own. And it was failing badly on both counts.

"I love them," she moaned. Was it really too late? A few weeks ago, Mandy had willingly gone with her, chattering a mile a minute about the dances her ballerina doll could do. Buddy had offered to share his favorite car with her. And Henry... oh, the baby. He batted those ridiculously long eyelashes at her as he nestled into her shoulder, tucked his thumb in his mouth, and fell asleep.

Her kids loved her, no matter how flawed.

And flawed she was.

How could she ever make it up to them, especially if the courts granted full custody to Dan?

✒

"SEE WHAT MS. FRAN GAVE ME?" Mandy held out a Christmas ornament.

Dan steeled his face as he took the ballerina angel from the little girl's hand. "It's pretty." But he knew what was coming next.

"She said it's for our Christmas tree." Mandy squared her shoulders, plopped both hands on her hips, and angled a glare upward. "How come we haven't put up our Christmas tree? Ms. Fran said Christmas is next week!"

"Uh, yeah. Sorry."

"Is it because it's Mama's job?"

Now there was an easy way out. Dan hesitated, tempted, but it wasn't fair to dump the blame on Dixie. The artificial tree lay in a box in the master closet with a small collection of ornaments. All of it was Dixie's from before they'd met, except for a few trinkets they'd added since.

He studied Mandy then spun the dancing angel from his finger by its tiny feet. The Christmas spirit was evading him this year, not that he'd ever been big into the holiday. He'd learned from Buddy's age that Santa favored Dave Junior just like Dad and Mom did.

How had he become the bringer of Christmas to three small kids? He had to step up to the plate, whether he felt like it or not. Wasn't this what the legal action was all about — stabilizing their young lives? Proving he loved them and would always be here for them?

Start with digging out the tree, Daniel John Ranta. Stream some Christmas music. Buy some presents. Sheesh, man. Be the adult here.

He stretched his hand toward Mandy. "Come on. Can you help me? We can do it right now."

She gave a little hop as her face brightened. "Really, Daddy? Right now?"

Dan's heart squeezed. She'd been the one telling the boys he wasn't their daddy ever since Thanksgiving, as though someone had to step into Dixie's shoes. Mandy hadn't slipped up often. "Really, baby. But we have to be quick or Henry will be rattling the gate at the bottom."

"Well, hurry up, then!" Mandy dashed for the stairs. "It's time we got some Christmas!"

Half an hour later, the silver tree with its blue and silver balls stood in the corner of the living room. The thing was pretty much self-decorating, and Mandy didn't seem to notice that he'd left the little box of personal decorations on a shelf, only bringing down the generic ones. The ones that wouldn't hurt so much to look at.

She stood in front of the tree, holding her new angel, obviously conflicted about where to hang it. Buddy stood beside her, staring thoughtfully at the blue spheres. Henry barreled over, yelling, "pretty!"

Dan grabbed the toddler before he pulled the whole thing over. "No touching, Henry." He needed to find the baby gate pieces Dixie had surrounded the tree with last year, when Henry'd been crawling.

"Daddy, hang car." Buddy thrust his favorite race car at Dan.

"If I do that, you can't play with it until after Christmas. That's a week away. Are you sure?"

Buddy eyed the ballerina angel Mandy had finally placed then nodded sharply. "Hang car. Please."

"Okay. I have to find a hook for it, or maybe some fishing line. Give me a minute." He carried the squirming toddler up the stairs under one arm and went in search of a roll of monofilament. It took a bit of creativity to hang the car somewhat level from one of the branches.

Buddy tucked his hands behind his back and beamed at the dangling vehicle. "Pretty," he said to Mandy.

"It's a dumb old car." She wrinkled her nose at him.

"No dumb."

"Be nice, Mandy. You have a special angel, and your brother has a special car. It works."

She huffed a sigh. "Daddy, is Mama coming home for Christmas? We should find her a special ornament, too. And one for you and Henry."

Dan's throat constricted. Sadie mentioned that Juanita had requested a later judicial appearance on Dixie's behalf, citing counseling and the appearance of change, but how much could he trust that she was putting in any effort?

He touched the bun on top of Mandy's head. Fran's doing, or maybe Ava's, for the dance practice. "I'm not sure, baby."

Come to Jesus, they'd said. *He'll make all things new. He'll give you peace and joy in the dark times.* What they hadn't told him was how dark the darkness would get. How long it would last. How much pain it would cause.

Mandy twirled away from under his hand on her head in some sort of pirouette.

Was a breakthrough truly coming? He prayed it for Dixie constantly, because it seemed only she could bring dawn into his own life.

It wasn't true. In his head, he knew it was Jesus' job, not Dixie's.

Mandy struck an arabesque, and Dan recognized the opening measures of *Angels We Have Heard on High* from the speakers. He held Henry close and listened to the words. Truly listened.

Angels we have heard on high sweetly singing o'er the plains, and the mountains in reply, echoing their joyous strains.

Then the triumphant: *Gloria in excelsis Deo!*

Didn't this all happen at night, too? He remembered the night Henry was born. Dixie had been in labor almost two whole days, and it had seemed like it would never end. Had it been the same for Jesus' mother, Mary?

Shepherds, why this jubilee? Why your joyous strains prolong? What the gladsome tidings be which inspire your heavenly song? Come to Bethlehem and see Him Whose birth the angels sing; come, adore on bended knee, Christ the Lord, the newborn King.

That long night had ended with the birth of the Savior. Lately, Dan had been so caught up in the issues of every day that he'd missed the wonder of the upcoming Christmas season. Missed remembering that Jesus had come to bring light out of darkness.

Mandy danced to the end of the carol, quite majestically for a little kid, if a dad could be so proud. Buddy lay on his back under the tree, looking up at his car. And little Henry snuggled against Dan's shoulder, fingering the frayed neck of his daddy's T-shirt.

How could he have almost let this opportunity slip by

without making sure his kids knew that Christmas was more than Santa, trees, and glitter?

He cleared his throat. "Hey, guys. Let's sit down in front of the tree. I want to tell you a story."

And tomorrow, he needed to go buy a nativity set from somewhere, something unbreakable, so the kids could see a representation of the Christmas story.

16

*D*ixie slipped into the darkened church at seven-fifteen, hoping she wasn't so late she'd miss seeing Mandy's dance. She'd planned to stand just inside the door, but there was plenty of room in the back pew, so why not have a seat? She'd be less conspicuous, and she'd done her best to camouflage herself anyway with a long dark coat and a black beanie over her tucked-up hair.

If someone recognized her, so what? It was a public service, Juanita had said. Anyone could go. She'd just make sure to slip out before Dan or the kids could see her. All she needed was a glimpse.

The first carol had been sung, and the two-and-three-year-olds made their way onto the stage. They lisped along to *Away in a Manger*. Dixie couldn't help smiling at their antics, some of the little ones so bashful as to be in tears, while others shouted and jumped off the platform in the middle of the song.

Then came the fours and fives. Dixie's heart clenched at

the sight of Buddy's soft blond curls as her little boy, her middle child, stood with his group, cupping his ear along with the others as they sang *Do You Hear What I Hear?* By the movement of his lips, he appeared to be a few words behind the other kids, but hey, he was trying. He remained focused on the adult leader crouching below the stage. Dixie's mama heart filled.

The leader — Ava Santoro — distributed small drums to the children. Uh oh. But the strains of *Little Drummer Boy* came through the speakers as the kids pounded uncertain rhythms.

Before she knew it, Buddy's class was finished. Dixie strained to see where her little boy would find a seat. She made out Dan's dark blond head off on the far side, leaning toward Buddy.

Dixie wanted to be beside them, to feel Dan's arm around her shoulders, to kiss Buddy's curls and tell him he did a good job, to revel in her baby reaching for her with both hands outstretched. How could she have thrown all that away?

A stir of air caught her attention as someone settled into the end of the row beside her. Dixie stiffened, glancing at the newcomer from beneath lowered lashes. Basil Santoro? She hadn't been this close to him since the night he'd run the police roadblock with her in the car and received a DUI, complete with jail time, for his efforts.

"Hey, Dixie." His elbow caught her arm, his voice low. "Long time no see... and in church, no less."

She edged away, trying for a little space between them, but now she was crowding the old man on the other side. "Same to you, in church," she whispered back.

Basil shrugged, poking his chin toward the front. "My nephews are up there. Promised my brother Marco I'd come. Besides, there's usually a great feed downstairs afterward, all kinds of cookies and squares. A single guy has to take free food where he can get it."

Yeah, no Christmas cookies for her. If she could escape this building with no one the wiser — besides Basil, apparently — she'd do it. "Don't tell anyone you saw me here."

He chuckled softly. "Still running and hiding, huh, Dix?"

She glowered at him in the dim light. "Aren't you?" Their brief liaison of eighteen months back hadn't all been her, that was for sure. He'd been a very willing participant.

"Dunno. My nonna and God have eyes everywhere, seems like."

What was that supposed to mean? But a shuffle from the stage caught her attention. A couple in long robes approached a door in the set. "May we get a room?" asked a young boy's voice.

The kid behind the door shook his head — or hers — it was hard to tell with the weird head covering. "There's no room." The door began to close then he peeked back out. "Sorry."

"But my wife is going to have her baby any time!"

"There's a stable over there, if you want. It's the best I can do." This time the door closed firmly. The spotlight on the door dimmed while the one across the stage brightened on a crude framework around cardboard animals overlooking a wooden manger.

The couple trudged toward it. Upon arrival, the girl tugged a doll out from under her top, wrapped it in a long strip of cloth, and laid it in the feeding box. Then both of them knelt beside it, staring.

Dixie shifted. She'd heard of the nativity story, of course. But, somehow on this December evening, it seemed closer than before. Maybe it was the fact that her own children weren't beside her. Maybe it was the dejected slump of the young couple's shoulders as they crossed the stage. Maybe it was the darkness and the background music and the hallowed hush in the auditorium.

Whatever it was, Dixie leaned forward slightly, watching with rapt attention. She heard the scrape as the inn door was dragged off stage, caught a glimpse of the swishing curtain. Then the spotlight brightened again on several kids kneeling beside cardboard sheep cutouts. One boy winced and held up his arm to block the light. Dixie pushed back a chuckle.

A third spotlight shone on a boy in the center of the stage, near the front. He pushed glasses up his nose, picked up a microphone, and began to sing. "'It came upon the midnight clear, that glorious song of old, from angels bending near the earth, to touch their harps of gold; "Peace on the earth, good will to men, from Heav'n's all-gracious King." The world in solemn stillness lay, to hear the angels sing.'"

The child couldn't be more than ten or eleven, but his voice rang with clear conviction.

Behind him, all the lights came up just enough for Dixie to see half a dozen little kids wearing white robes, angel wings, and halos, begin to dance, Mandy the smallest one. Dixie held her breath as her daughter twirled and leaped in formation with the others while the boy's voice soared.

"'Still through the cloven skies they come with peaceful wings unfurled, and still their heav'nly music floats o'er all the weary world...'"

The words sank into Dixie's heart. They spoke of suffering, of life's crushing loads, of heavy toil, but they also spoke of a love-song brought by the angels.

"'Look now! for glad and golden hours come swiftly on the wing. Oh, rest beside the weary road, and hear the angels sing!'"

Basil's elbow broke her reverie. "Kid's got a good voice, doesn't he?"

She blinked. "He's amazing."

"Sam Diaz. Although I'm not sure if his stepdad adopted him yet, in which case he'd be Sam Sheridan."

Sheridan. Weren't they Dan's neighbors, just down the block and around the corner? They'd once been *her* neighbors, too, before she blew everything.

Sam exited the stage as a chorus began singing *Angels We Have Heard on High*. This was the dance Mandy'd been so excited about a few weeks ago. And rightly so. The little girl did just as good as the biggest angel, and better than most. Not that Dixie was adding up points. Except she was.

She'd wanted to dance as a kid. Mom had rolled her eyes, and that had been the end of it. Dixie'd been no more accommodating with Mandy. But Dan? He'd find a way to make the little girl's dreams come true, because Dan was a good guy like that.

Why again had Dixie kept telling him no when he asked her to marry him? Why did she feel the need to keep the upper hand? Because it had done her no good. He'd called her bluff and filed for permanent solo custody in an effort to cut her right out of the equation.

She couldn't blame him. She'd been an idiot... and now it was too late. Or was it?

⌇

"You did amazing, Mandy-girl. Good job!" Dan gave the little girl a high five and watched the beam spread across her face. Then she looked around the sanctuary as though seeking someone specific.

I know what you're thinking, baby.

Mandy sighed, her delight dimmer. She turned back to Buddy and hugged him. "You sang good."

Buddy pushed away from his sister. "Sam better."

Linnea patted Buddy's shoulder. "Sam's a lot bigger than you, and I know he takes voice lessons. When you're his age, you could sing as good as him, too, if you practice. Like an angel."

He shrugged her hand away, a scowl settling on his little face.

Linnea caught Dan's eye, but he shook his head. How was he supposed to know what was going on in the kids' heads? Sure, they noticed all the families together in the audience, with the moms taking pride in their kids' performances. He couldn't keep them away from other families to protect their tender hearts. It wouldn't work, anyway.

Logan leaned around Linnea. "Shall we go downstairs and get some of those amazing cookies? You haven't seen anything until you've seen the Christmas concert spread down there. Why do you think we came home from Seattle for Christmas?"

"Mr. Tony made struffoli," Mandy informed Logan. "They're super yummy. He let me try one."

"Handy having a live-in cook?" Logan's eyes danced as he looked at Dan.

"Sure is. Takes the strain off of early morning plowing, too, but there hasn't been a ton of snow yet this winter."

Linnea rested her hand on Dan's arm. "I'm glad you found a solution that works."

"For this winter, anyway. He'll be opening up Antonio's later in spring and finding his own place. Meanwhile, though, he's been a godsend."

His sister laughed. "Jasmine told me her parents were quite put out that Marietta managed to get out of Tony living with her."

Dan found the Santoro matriarch across the space. Marietta bossed several small kids, shooing them toward the basement stairs. "She seems to be doing all right. And she was right — I needed Tony around more than she did."

Logan took the older two by the hand and merged with the people exiting the sanctuary. Linnea reached for Henry, but the toddler burrowed deeper against Dan's shoulder. "I'm sorry Mom and Dad didn't come tonight," she said, dropping her hands.

"Yeah, me, too. I'm sorry she let him bully her out of coming. I know she wanted to, but you know Dad."

His sister grimaced. "All too well. We'll just have to keep praying for them and for our esteemed brother."

"Yeah."

She glanced around as though gauging where the kids were. "And... Dixie. How are things?"

Linnea and Logan had arrived from Edmonds last night for their winter college break. They'd been busy with finals, and his sister hadn't called as often as usual in the past few weeks.

Dan jiggled Henry gently, but the little guy seemed asleep. "Radio silence, but I hear she's getting some counseling from Juanita Ramirez."

"That's great!"

"Yeah. It is." Too bad he didn't know what to do with the information. Sadie had approved the delay of the custody interview on Dan's behalf, so there was that. But what did it all really mean? No clue.

He stepped into the aisle behind his sister, and they worked their way into the church basement with a hundred or more others.

"She was here! I saw her," Fran said from behind Dan somewhere. "Back row."

Up ahead, he saw Logan loading a plate while two small kids pointed at goodies from the decorated tables.

"All I saw in the back row was Basil," countered Ava's voice.

"He's home for Christmas? I guess Aunt Grace will be happy to have all her chicks in the nest."

"I guess so." Ava heaved a sigh.

Dan didn't know why he was paying attention to the Santoro cousins' gossip. It wasn't like Basil's whereabouts were any of his business. If Dixie had run off to Seattle after Thanksgiving, maybe things would be different, but she hadn't. She'd stayed in the same city as her children. As Dan.

"Where did he disappear to, then? You'd think he'd want Nonna to note his presence in church."

Ava laughed. "No one thinks like Basil, and you know it. Especially if he was in church with *her*."

Who'd they seen with their cousin? Dan turned and caught sight of the two women not far away. Fran's hand flew up to cover her mouth as her eyes grew wide.

Dan's stomach soured. That could only mean one thing. Dixie had been here... with Basil. Sure, she'd known better than to approach him or the kids with the temporary injunction in place, but she hadn't been smart enough to come alone.

Dixie was *his*. Basil had no right to horn in. Dixie had no right to look elsewhere. Were the legal proceedings Dan had started only enabling her to rid herself of three little burdens — and one big one — so she could be free as a bird? Had she been seeing Basil all this time, making trips to Seattle, or him coming here?

How *could* she?

"Dan? You okay?" His sister's hand touched his arm.

He shook his head and turned away, breaking eye contact with Fran. "No. Not really. Henry's asleep, and he weighs twice what you'd think. I need to get him home to bed." He started to fake a yawn, but it turned into the real thing. "We're supposed to get some snow overnight, so I might need to get up early to plow."

"Do you want us to bring the other kids by in a bit? They're just getting started."

Logan steered Mandy and Buddy to a table where a bunch of men sat. Jacob, Nathan, Peter, and others Logan knew. They were Dan's friends, too, from prayer breakfast. These guys could talk until daybreak if left to their own devices.

Dan shook his head. "I'll give the kids a few minutes, but they'll come home with me. They're my responsibility, not yours."

And, apparently, not Dixie's, either.

17

*D*ixie toyed with the straps of her handbag and watched Basil settle in across the booth at Morley's Café. He'd come. She hadn't been sure he would and hadn't dared stick around long enough to be certain.

On the other hand, hadn't he lost his license? "How come you're driving, anyway? I thought your driver's license was revoked for two years."

He skewered her with narrowed dark eyes. "There are ways around that."

"Don't tell me you drove all this way illegally!"

"Dix, you're the last person to tell me what's right and what's wrong."

The waitress came, bored, popping her gum.

"Plum cheesecake and chamomile tea," Dixie ordered.

Basil shook his head before ordering huckleberry cheesecake with black coffee.

She looked down. Her fingers snapped and unsnapped her purse, nervous as all get out. Why? This was just Basil.

"I've got an ignition interlock device, okay? It's perfectly legal for me to drive with that stupid thing." His elbows hit the table as he leaned closer. "Don't pretend you don't know what it is."

Dixie tilted her chin. "I wasn't born yesterday." And she hung around with far too many people who'd sported a DUI or two.

"So, you really broke it off with Ranta? Didn't see that coming."

"He became a Christian—"

"Of course." Basil snapped his fingers as he leaned back. "That would do it. Now he's too good for you, right? Just like all the other holier-than-thou people we both know."

"He was always a good guy."

Basil laughed.

"No, really, he was. And getting into this church thing... well, he's even better than before."

"I don't even hear sarcasm."

"Because it's not." Dixie sighed. "You say he's too good for me, but it's true. Not because he looks down on me, but because he's just that amazing."

"And here I thought we were going out for *coffee*—" he air-quoted the word "—as a possible prelude for more interesting activities. But you're here to tell me how terrific your ex is? I should've stayed and had Tony's struffoli and Adriana's sugar cookies in the church basement. At least then I'd have known I wasn't picking anyone up."

"You're rude."

"Now that's the pot calling the kettle black." His dark eyes narrowed on hers. "What do you want from me, Dixie? A fling? Something more? Or just a cup of insipid brewed herbs?"

She opened her mouth and closed it again as the waitress deposited cheesecake in front of each of them followed by their drinks. "I thought you could explain the attraction of the whole faith thing."

"Are you kidding me?" Basil forked in a bite of cheesecake. "You do remember you're talking to the black sheep of the family, right? The one who walked away?"

"I know who you are, Basil Santoro. And I also see you back in Bridgeview for Christmas with your family, even coming to a church program because your nephews were in it, so I don't think you're as immune as you pretend. What's the secret?"

He shook his head and ate half his cheesecake.

Dixie picked at hers. It was good, sweet and creamy, but her mouth seemed to turn everything sour. Words. Food.

"Dix, why not ask Dan this question? He's obviously found something in religion that neither you nor I have."

"I can't talk to him. He... he's cut me off. He filed for custody."

Basil's eyebrows shot up. "Of Henry?"

"Of all three."

"But he's not — that's crazy."

"You'd think so, wouldn't you? But he's a great father, and he loves the kids." Dixie mashed a bite of cheesecake against the edge of the plate. "Whereas I'm a terrible mother, and I have no idea how to show love."

Basil held up both hands. "Dix, you're way above my pay grade here. You want to know why people are attracted to religion? I guess some find peace and satisfaction. Some find belonging. I have no idea."

"If you had peace and satisfaction and belonging, how

could you turn your back on it? You have a great family, unlike me. My mom's a piece of work, and yours is a dream."

"There's only so much peace some of us can handle before we feel strangled. Belonging to the Santoro family can kill a guy with claustrophobia. I'm not sure how else to describe it."

At least he was giving her a somewhat thoughtful answer. It was more than she'd expected. She sipped her tea. "I don't get it."

"Neither does anyone else."

"All I can think is someone broke your heart."

His eyebrows shot up.

"No, really. A woman, most likely." Dixie studied him. "Or maybe God."

"You're talking about Him as though He's real."

"Isn't He?"

"You're totally talking to the wrong person here. I've got nothing for you, Dix. I don't have answers, and I don't have a fling in me for someone asking those kinds of questions. Talk to Ranta."

"I've been getting some counseling from Juanita Ramirez."

"Pastor Tomas's wife?" Basil flung both hands in the air. "See? You don't need me for anything."

"She thinks..." Dixie paused. "She thinks I need Jesus."

"Well, of course, she thinks that. She's paid to. Sheesh, Dix, use your brain."

"I've been thinking for myself for twenty-five years, and look where that got me. I've been doing a really lousy job. I barely got my high school diploma. I've birthed three kids by three different men. I've been stone drunk more times than I can count. My best job has been barmaid, and even that isn't so great lately because I can't handle the advances of the regulars in there anymore." She leaned on the table and stared into Basil's eyes. "Tell me where in that I've proved I can chart my own course."

Basil rocked his chair back onto two legs, cup of coffee in one hand. He shook his head. "Hard to argue with that litany."

"So, it seems God could hardly do a worse job of running my life than I'm doing on my own."

"You've got me there."

"So, I should give God a chance? What do I have to do?"

"Jeepers, Dix. Ask someone else!"

"I'm asking you."

"Right, well, the pat answer is you pray and ask God to forgive your sins. You know, all the bad stuff you've done. And then you're a happy jolly Christian and your life is just peachy perfect from then on and forevermore."

"That simple?"

"That's what they say." The front legs of Basil's chair thudded against the floor again. "But how would I know? I was the little kid who bought in, hook, line, and sinker. And it wasn't enough for me. Seems to work for lots of people, though."

"Really? Just pray and say sorry?"

"Yup. And if you believe your life will be smooth and perfect after that, you're more naive than I'd give you credit for."

Dixie thought that through. "It didn't work that way for Dan. I think his life is harder than before."

"See?"

"But part of that's my fault. If I'd just given in sooner, we'd be good."

"So, say your prayers and go crawling back to Ranta." Basil pushed back his chair and rose to his feet. "And this religious and relationship advice is free. You're getting what you paid for, don't forget. I'll pick up the tab for dessert on my way out."

She watched him stride away. He dropped a twenty at the till, waved away the change, and marched out to his car. Though she couldn't see him, she imagined him angrily giving the ignition interlock device a breathalyzer test before the headlights came on. His car peeled out of the lot, sliding a little on the icy corner.

Basil's answers lined up with Juanita's. With Dan's. With the little bit of Bible she'd read.

Dixie took another sip of her tea. Was that all it took, then? Just a little prayer? She couldn't do this to impress Dan and get her kids back. If God was everything they said He was, He'd see through it, and she'd have done another sin she'd need to repent from.

It was almost enough to make her not even want to try, because she was pretty sure she'd never be able to be perfect. In no time flat she'd be back at square one. But, wasn't that true of Dan, too? He'd lost his temper a few times since he'd found Jesus. For all she'd told Basil Dan was practically perfect, she knew he wasn't. Not quite. And Juanita had told Dixie some things she'd done that weren't all that great since she'd believed. So, they just prayed — again — and God forgave them — again — and it was all okay?

Yeah, she needed to talk to Juanita some more, but it was Christmas week, and they didn't have anything scheduled until afterward since Dan's attorney had accepted the delay.

Maybe she could try reading the Bible. Because she really wanted to get to the reality in that part Linnea had told her about.

'Let's prepare a great feast and celebrate. For this beloved son of mine was once dead, but now he's alive again. Once he was lost, but now he is found!' And everyone celebrated with overflowing joy.

She wanted *that* kind of party.

"YOU CAN'T KEEP my grandchildren away from me at Christmas!" Eunice blustered over the phone.

Dan rubbed his forehead. Where had she been for the past month? She hadn't called once. "You'll have to talk to my attorney. She'll be in the office again on the twenty-seventh."

"But that's—"

"After Christmas. I know." Not his fault she'd waited until the twenty-third to make a stink. He turned away from the blissfully domestic scene in the living room where the two older kids decorated race car coloring sheets he'd printed from online. Buddy's was covered in bold red and blue strokes, while Mandy's pink-and-purple creation sparkled from her glitter gel pens.

"Dan, I don't know what you're trying to prove."

"Prove?" The word exploded out before he could stop it. The nerve of the woman. "I'm trying to provide stability for three small kids. It's not about Dixie. It's not about me. It's about the children."

"Pshaw. They're not even your kids. Probably Henry isn't, either."

He'd had a qualm or two back then, for sure, and he'd do the paternity test if the courts required it. But how could there be any doubt, really? The toddler was created in Dan's image.

"Eunice, I appreciate that you care for the children—" wasn't that a laugh? "—but I have to ask you not to call again. The situation is in the hands of the courts, and their decision will be final. If you have anything to add to the debate, you will need to present it to Ms. Guthrie at Dawson and Banks."

"But, Dan—!"

"Goodbye, Eunice." He tapped the button to end the call and took a deep breath, a cleansing breath, before turning back to the room.

Tony sat beside Buddy with a coloring sheet of his own, matching the little boy's bold colors while remaining in the lines. He looked up and raised his eyebrows at Dan.

Mandy arranged her glitter pens in a neat row as she cast furtive glances at Dan.

Thankfully, the baby was asleep.

He swallowed his frustration as best he could and crossed the space, kneeling beside her chair. "That's a beautiful car, Mandy. So... sparkly."

She scowled at him. "I want Grandma."

"I'm sorry."

"I want Mama." Her lip turned down in a full pout as

she crossed her arms over her chest and slumped in her chair.

"Me, too, baby." He reached for her, but she jerked her shoulder to come between them. His hand dropped along with his heart.

"Then where is she? And why do you use big words to make her stay away?"

Buddy dropped his crayon and stared between them. Tony took a deep breath and kept coloring, gaze on his paper, lip between his teeth.

Lord? I could use some help here.

"I know it's hard, baby. Your mama is going through some stuff. We need to pray for her, okay?"

"But I need her."

Dan nodded.

Buddy slipped off his chair, rounded the table, and wrapped his arms around Dan's neck. Dan held the little boy tight.

Was he really doing the right thing? Was it better for Mandy to have her mom as an erratic presence in her life... or not to have her at all? Even as he wavered, he remembered Dixie locking her daughter in an empty house. He remembered Mandy's terror that had lingered for weeks. The nightmares.

No, he had to follow through. Mandy was not quite six. She couldn't understand the long-term repercussions of Dixie's issues.

It had been seven months since Dan had first believed. He'd been so hopeful. He'd envisioned coming home and leading Dixie to Jesus the same day. Then he'd been sure it would only be a matter of time. Yeah, seven months wasn't eternity, but it felt like it. It was a solid third of their toddler's life.

Slowly, reluctantly, he'd come to realize it might never happen. That Dixie might choose to remain mired in her old life and never join him in the new one. If she'd only stayed responsible, engaged with the kids, he'd be happy to co-parent with her. Well, not happy exactly, but he'd deal with it. Lots of couples managed to provide a decent upbringing for their kids even when they separated.

They were at an impasse. He could give up his faith and invite Dixie back into their home, into his bed. He could call Jesus a failed experiment and claim Dixie back from Basil.

But he couldn't. Not when he'd received life itself. Peace, even in the midst of storms. A hope and a promise to see him through the darkest night. The blackout seemed complete. No hint of dawn brought even the faintest glow to the horizon, but the promise of Jesus was still present. *I'll never leave you nor forsake you.*

A tear trickled down Mandy's cheek.

This time when Dan reached for her, she tumbled into his arms. He rocked back with the impact and cradled both kids tight against his chest.

his is the worst Christmas of my life!" Dixie glared at her mother. So much for a lovely — or at least peaceful — interlude in her ugly life. The holiday was supposed to be for family, but Dan's lawyer wouldn't let her see the kids, and her mother had a new flavor-of-the-month.

They were all over each other. It wasn't even amusing. Mom stood in the doorway, the guy's arms groping around her from behind while he nuzzled her neck. He couldn't be much older than Dixie. Ugh.

"Then go home to your empty apartment. You're just a loser, anyway."

Didn't she know it? No matter how much she tried to dodge the knowledge, it slammed her at every turn. Dixie pivoted, grabbed her purse and jacket, and stomped into the corridor of Mom's apartment building. The door snapped shut behind her. The deadbolt clacked.

In the lobby, Dixie shrugged on her faux fur coat and stared out at the softly falling snow. If Dan wasn't out plowing, he would be soon. Maybe he'd have the kids outside building a snowman or something. She could drive by the house and see.

She wasn't supposed to, according to the legal letter. But wasn't there such a thing as innocent until proven guilty? Just because Dan had a temporary injunction until the court appearance didn't mean anything.

Okay, it did. If she got caught stalking the house, it could close the case against her. But she had to see the kids. Were they safe? Happy? Had they already forgotten her?

Dixie inched down the icy street to the bottom of the hill and turned left onto Water Street. One drive-by. That would have to be enough. She slowed as the small two-story house came into view, nestled between its neighbors. Dan's truck was parked outside beside a nondescript black car. His sister's? The main windows were at the back of the house. There was nothing to see here.

She turned the corner at the end of the block then turned east again on the next street up. The route took her out of the neighborhood past Bridgeview Bakery and Bistro. Closed for Christmas Day, of course, not that she'd go in even it wasn't. The owner, Hailey North, despised Dixie as much as Dixie scorned her. The woman was after anything with a Y chromosome.

On a whim, she turned up the next street, a short one that ended in the church parking lot. She stared at the building for a few minutes. A couple of inches of untouched snow covered the lot and the front steps, proving no one had been by. And why would they? Even Juanita and Tomas had a family to spend Christmas with. Everyone did but her.

Dixie rested her forehead on the steering wheel as tears burned her eyes. Was she destined to spend the rest of her life alone? Dan said he loved her, but it wasn't enough. Not for him. Not for her. Her mother was supposed to love her, but that was a joke, wasn't it?

Tanisha and Billie said a mother's love was the most important. If Dixie was this wrecked at her mother's selfishness, she had to believe her own actions were doing the same thing to her own kids. Was it an unbreakable cycle? Or did she have a choice?

Had the prodigal son had a choice? He'd made one, even though he wasn't sure how it would end. He'd taken a chance and put his future in his father's hands. He'd expected, at best, to become a servant. He hadn't expected the party.

'This beloved son of mine was once dead, but now he's alive again. Once he was lost, but now he is found!' And everyone celebrated with overflowing joy.

Dixie felt dead. Lost. She fumbled in her purse for a tissue to stem the tide.

A tap on her window sent her scrambling, heart pounding. Who? What? Her pulse calmed when she recognized Juanita through the steamed-up window. She pressed the button to lower the glass.

"Are you all right, sweetie?" Juanita's coat was wrapped around her tiny frame, but not done up. Her hair had gathered a few snowflakes, but underneath it, her eyes were tender and her smile genuine.

"Yes." Dixie hiccuped. "No."

Juanita pointed over her shoulder at the church. "Want to come in for a cup of tea?"

"I — you have your family. Don't worry about me."

"Tomas is capable of clearing the table. Have you eaten?"

Dixie remembered the take-out turkey dinner her mom had ordered. "Yeah."

"You sure? We have lots of leftovers."

"I couldn't."

"Tea, then?" Juanita held up a plastic-film-covered plate. "I grabbed some cookies on my way out the door."

Dixie glanced across the parking lot, following the trail of footsteps to a row of houses over on Cedar. "You can't give up your Christmas Day for a loser like me." The pastor's wife must have seen her car from the window and come over. Who would do that?

"Come on. Let's talk." Juanita tugged open the car door.

Dixie pressed the button to slide the window up, turned off the ignition, and followed the pastor's wife to the church's side door.

Juanita flipped on a few light switches before filling and plugging in the kettle. "Chamomile?"

Standing uncertainly in the middle of the reception area, Dixie nodded.

"Tell me about your day, sweetie."

"I miss my kids," she whispered. "And I want things to change."

"What kinds of things?"

She took a deep breath. "I guess it has to start with me. I don't want to be a loser anymore. My mom always made sure I knew I didn't measure up, and I guess I proved her right. But I don't want to be that person anymore. Can someone really change?"

"Let me tell you about Jesus. That's what He does. He takes people who are at the end of themselves and gives them a new purpose. He makes them into something new."

"What does He want from me in return?"

"Just your heart, sweetie. Your trust." Juanita poured the boiling water over teabags in two mugs. "Here, take the cookies into my office, and I'll bring these."

Her heart. Her trust. Was that what Dan had given Jesus? It seemed like it.

"WANT TO TALK ABOUT IT?" Logan leaned back in the armchair in Dan's living room. It was the evening of Christmas Day, and the kids were finally asleep after a tumultuous day. Tony was out at one of his relatives' homes — Dan didn't know whose. And Linnea was catching up with Jasmine and Nathan.

Dan poured a tall glass of pop for each of them and handed one to his brother-in-law. "I think things are okay. Ish." He dropped into the recliner beside the tree.

"Ish?" Logan saluted him with the glass by way of thanks.

"Yeah. I know I need to proceed with this, but it's been kind of rough. That whole thing where she came to the church concert then went out with Basil kills me."

"Basil dropped by his sister's in a foul mood less than an hour later."

Hope sprang in Dan's chest, but he quelled it. "That's the problem with Bridgeview. Everyone knows everything."

Logan chuckled. "Too true. Bro, I've been thinking

about what you told me at Thanksgiving, what Jacob said to you."

Dan's eyebrows shot up. "Yeah? Still makes me mad when I think about it. I kept going to the men's prayer breakfast — and I'm thankful for Eden sitting with the kids — but forgive me if I don't especially want to hang out with the guy one on one."

"He has a point."

"Not you, too." Dan's head sagged back against the headrest. "It makes no sense."

"You decided that the only sensible solution was to marry Dixie. Am I right?"

He gave his brother-in-law a *duh* look.

"But... did you ask God?"

Dan gave his head a quick shake. "Of course, I asked God. I've asked Him a billion times to get Dixie's attention and make her come around."

"That's not what I asked."

"What other question is there?"

"Did you ask God what He really wants, even if it's not marriage to Dixie? What if He has a completely different solution, but you're too Velcroed to your own obviously-correct-opinion to see what He really has for you?"

"What else could there be?"

"That's not the point. The point is, are you willing to give God room to show you?"

Dan opened his mouth in protest and snapped it shut again. Could Logan be right? Was he so fixated on his own solution that he couldn't even see anything else?

"There's a great psalm — have you been reading those? — lots of good stuff in the Psalms. This one is pretty short."

Logan thumbed his phone on and tapped around. "May I read it to you?"

"Uh, sure."

"Okay. It's Psalm 37. Been loving The Passion Translation lately. Here we go. 'Don't follow after the wicked ones or be jealous of their wealth. Don't think for a moment they're better off than you. They and their short-lived success will soon shrivel up and quickly fade away like grass clippings in the hot sun.'"

Logan looked up with a grin. "Those grass clippings are when I started thinking about you, and then I couldn't get you out of my mind while I read the rest."

"Go on."

"'Keep trusting in the Lord and do what is right in his eyes. Fix your heart on the promises of God and you will be secure, feasting on his faithfulness.'" Logan paused.

"Sounds good. What promises do you think he's talking about there?"

"Let me keep going. 'Make God the utmost delight and pleasure of your life, and he will provide for you what you desire most.'"

"Yeah, that." Dan pointed at Logan's phone. "What I desire most? A Christ-centered marriage with Dixie."

Logan held up his hand like a stop sign. "There's more. 'Give God the right to direct your life, and as you trust him along the way you'll find he pulled it off perfectly! He will appear as your righteousness, as sure as the dawning of a new day. He will manifest as your justice, as sure and strong as the noonday sun.'"

Give God the right to direct your life. Dan winced. He'd jumped into this faith business with both feet, reveling in the joy of Jesus' love. He'd felt absolute certainty that the perfect life was his for the taking... and that he knew exactly how it would look.

Logan's voice lowered. "'Quiet your heart in his presence and pray; keep hope alive as you long for God to come through for you.'" His eyes scanned the phone then shrugged and flicked it off. "That's the basic idea."

"Why would this marriage not be God's will? That doesn't even make sense. How could anything be better for our kids? For us?"

His brother-in-law's eyes shone in sympathy. "I can't answer that, bro. But you know how a little kid holds on tight to their trinket, sure it's the most amazing thing ever, even though their parent wants to give them something bigger and better?"

"Buddy did that today," Dan mused. "He wanted those little race cars from his stocking so much I could hardly convince him to open his main gift."

"Which contained a three-speed ride-in car. Left to his own devices, he'd have missed it."

Dan laughed, eyeing the large toy sitting over by the patio door. Buddy would have so much fun with that thing in the backyard and on neighborhood walks. Even ripping around inside the house with its limited space, the kid had sported a beaming smile the rest of the day, the little cars forgotten. "He was sure surprised. It was fun giving him something he didn't even know he wanted." The words registered in his mind and thudded into his heart. "Like that, huh?"

"Maybe." Logan lifted a shoulder. "The thing is, we don't know, if we don't let go of our human-sized dreams. We have to trust that God's a good, good father. If you had a keyboard here, I'd play that song for you. Look it up on YouTube, bro. Chris Tomlin."

"I know the one. Yeah, I'll listen to it again. I like it."

"Please don't get me wrong. I'm just a guy like you, and I can't think of anything better for you than a whole, complete family. I felt strongly that I needed to come talk to you. Ask you if you'd really put the situation in God's hands, totally and completely. Because, if you do, He'll give you what's best. Not what you think is best, but what He knows."

Dan gulped. "That's a little scary."

"I hear you, bro."

"Because what if it's not Dixie? What if she doesn't ever come to faith and ask Jesus into her life? What then?"

Logan's eyes gleamed with sympathy as he met Dan's gaze. "That's where the trusting comes in. Have to ask you something else."

"What?" Dan braced himself.

"Because on the one side, you're taking legal action to solidify custody, but on the other, you haven't given up on Dixie. How does that fit together?"

He huffed out a breath and ran his hand through his hair. "It's a big risk, I guess. I just want to shake up her world, make her wake up and see what she's doing."

"So, you're counting on her coming through, so you can drop the custody case?"

"I guess. Does that sound lame? Stupid?"

"It could backfire."

Dan closed his eyes and leaned back. "I'm beginning to think it will. She went out with *Basil*."

"What then? If she settles down with some other guy, like Basil, maybe, would you be open to letting her take the kids?"

His chest tore apart in pain. "God can't ask that of me. The kids—" his voice broke. "They deserve better."

"What if it's God's best?"

Dan stumbled to his feet. "I don't know how you can say that. You said he didn't stay with Dixie long. That can't be what's happening."

"Pray, bro. Pray and make sure your heart is in line with God's. That you're really ready to give God complete control of your future. Yours, and Mandy's, and Buddy's, and Henry's."

"You don't know what you're asking."

Logan's arm squeezed Dan's shoulder for a few seconds. "I'm headed off to find Linnea now. Trust me. We are praying for you countless times a day. All of you."

"Thanks." *I think.*

The cold night air swirled in as Logan departed.

Dan dropped back into his chair and rested his head in his hands, elbows braced on his knees.

It's always darkest before dawn. He'd heard that saying countless times. But, what if this time, daybreak never came?

God! I need You!

19

*D*ixie leaned over the table, setting a beer in front of each guy. They were getting an eye-full at the same time, thanks to her low-cut uniform. A hand slid around her bottom and fingered the hem of her much-too-short, much-too-snug skirt.

She sidled out of the way, and the guy chuckled. "Playing hard to get, sweetheart?"

"Not just playing," she shot back, straightening.

The men erupted into laughter.

"Can I get you anything else?"

"Sure can," he drawled with a wink.

If she hadn't already set all the steins on the table, she might *accidentally* spill one in his lap. "From the menu."

"We're good for now," one of the others said.

As Dixie turned away, the guy's hand caught her leg. "For now."

"Get your dirty hands off me." Oh, no. Had she really said that? The bar seemed far too quiet, her voice far too loud.

The guy's look hardened and his fingers tightened. That would leave a bruise. Even if she'd been looking for a pickup, he would never have been it.

"Having troubles?" Seth appeared at her elbow. "I need to talk to you, Dixie."

Seth? She'd only seen him a few times since that first night at Billie and Jared's, and they'd never sat down just to talk. She let herself be led away, not glancing back as he guided her to the entry. "I didn't see you in there."

"I just came in." Seth searched her eyes. "Are you okay? You don't have to put up with unwanted advances, even here."

"That's where you're wrong." Kristoff's chilly voice interrupted. "You said you were up for this, Dixie. Said you needed the income, including the tips. You're not acting like someone who needs money."

Dixie took a deep breath and looked up at her boss. "That guy gives me the creeps."

"It's not just that one guy, and you know it. Customers have been complaining about your cold shoulder ever since you came back to work. What's gotten into you?"

Dan. Dan and Jesus. Dixie took a deep breath.

"Dude." Seth stepped in front of her. "You're nothing better than a pimp if that's all the value you place in your waitstaff."

Kristoff's bushy eyebrows met in the middle as he stabbed a beefy finger in Seth's chest. "No one asked you."

"Please..." Dixie's voice came out a squeak.

"You with him?" Her boss looked at her even as he kept a hand on Seth.

"Um, not exactly. I mean, I know him, but—"

"Get out." Kristoff shoved Seth at the door. "Don't come back."

"Not without her."

No. This was a bad time for Seth's chivalry... or was it? Maybe he was giving her the opening she needed. Since her meeting with Juanita yesterday and the prayers she'd prayed, she'd dreaded coming back to work tonight even more than she already had been.

Dixie straightened, not that she came past Kristoff's burly chest even so. "I quit. I just need to go get my stuff, and I'm out of here. Mail me my paycheck."

"There's no need for that nonsense." Kristoff rolled his eyes. "Get back in there and do your job. And step it up a notch, will you?"

"The lady says she quits."

"And I told *you* to get lost."

Seth was going to have to hold his own. Dixie ducked under Kristoff's arm then strode through the bar to the staff room at the rear. Decision made, she didn't want to take the time to change her clothes, but there was also no way she wanted to experience twenty below after midnight with so little on. She shimmied out of the uniform and dropped it on the floor then donned her jeans and sweat-shirt, tugged on her boots, and grabbed her jacket and purse.

Dixie hesitated. Her car was parked out back. Seth was in the front, if he hadn't already left. No way did she want to traverse the crowded lounge if she didn't have to. Back door it was.

Her hands shook as she stabbed the key at the ignition. She was crazy. She needed this job. Needed it to keep paying her share of Tanisha's rent. For clothes and makeup. Fuel for her car.

She backed out of the parking spot and navigated around to the front of the building, but there was no sign of Seth in the softly falling snow. She needed to thank him for his intervention, even though it had brought everything to a peak before she was ready. She could have flirted with the stupid customer, cowed to Kristoff, and kept the job she hated for another week or two until she'd found something different once the Christmas rush was over. On the other hand, what was done was done, and it had been coming.

Why hadn't she talked to Juanita about her work yesterday? Asked for advice? Surely a pastor's wife wouldn't have told her to keep a sleazy job, though.

Dixie drove the dozen blocks to Tanisha's apartment and climbed the stairs only to find the wreath backwards on the door. Great. Her friend was "entertaining." Dixie pivoted and marched back toward her car just as Seth pulled into the lot. What was he doing here?

He rolled down his window. "Good. You made it home. Just checking."

Not someone else with ulterior motives. She clutched her red handbag to her chest. "I'm fine."

He angled his head to one side. "But it looks like you're leaving again."

"Tanisha is... occupied."

Seth laughed. "Figures. Want to go for a coffee? One of the fast-food places, maybe."

"I hate coffee."

This time his laugh came from the gut. "You what? I've seen you drink it several times."

"Helps sober me up. Doesn't mean I like it." If anything, she associated it with a hangover. Like that made it appealing?

"Tea then. Or hot chocolate. Or ginger ale. Whatever."

Dixie studied him. "Okay." She dropped her keys back in her purse, rounded his car, climbed in, and fingered snowflakes out of her hair. "I've got nothing better to do."

Seth turned toward Division Street and glanced across at her. "I went into Kristoff's hoping to see you tonight."

"If you think me getting in your car means anything besides coffee, let me out at the corner."

He shook his head. "Relax. I'm not after your virtue."

She didn't have any, anyway. "What then?"

"Remember I told you I'd been religious once?"

Dixie's ears perked up. "Yeah. What happened?"

"God's got a sense of humor, is all I can say."

"What do you mean?"

"It means I spent Christmas with my family and came to my senses. I don't know if you're familiar with the Bible story about the prodigal son, but I—"

"I do know it! I love that one, especially the bit about everyone celebrating his return with overflowing joy."

Seth angled into a brightly lit parking lot. "You've read it?"

"My ex's sister told me about it, and I looked it up. That was a few weeks ago, and I've read it a pile of times since. It's just such a hopeful story for someone who's made as big a mess of her life as that son did."

He turned toward her, leaving the car idling. "I hear you. There's a lot of hope in it. There's a lot of hope in the Bible as a whole. I can't believe I just shut it all out of my life for so long. I know you were talking about your ex finding Jesus, and I needed to tell you—"

"I found Him."

"You what?"

"Yesterday. I was having a really bad day." She closed her eyes, wincing. "My mother's a hot mess, so I drove by Dan's, hoping for a glimpse of the kids, but no such luck. Then I found myself in the church parking lot. I've been seeing a counselor who happens to be a pastor's wife about how to handle this custody stuff with my kids, and I don't know why I went to the church on Christmas afternoon. I mean, the doors were locked. No one was there."

Seth waited.

"Except she saw me out her kitchen window and came over through the snow and unlocked the door and invited me in. We talked. I prayed." Dixie shivered. "I have no idea what to do now, especially since I don't have a job anymore."

"Knock on your ex's door and walk back in?"

"There's legal stuff in motion. I think I could be arrested for doing that." It almost seemed worth the risk, but... no. She might've been a believer for under forty-eight hours, but she knew enough not to jump in like that.

"That's a tough spot to be in. Is that what you want, though?" Seth reached across the center console and covered her hands with his. "Or just a fresh start?"

She tugged free. "My kids? Dan? Yeah. That's what I want." Could she have another chance, though?

Seth sighed. "I like you, Dixie. We've got so much in common."

"Don't start. This isn't a good time for me in any way. I

have to get my head screwed on straight. I mean, I've started, but I'm just far enough along to see how long the road really is." She swallowed hard. "I'm not giving up on Dan and the kids. Not yet. Maybe never. I don't know, but I can't make those kinds of decisions right now."

"I get it. I do." Seth thumbed over his shoulder to the brightly lit restaurant behind them. "Let's go get that coffee, or whatever you're having."

Dixie pushed the car door open and stepped out into several inches of fresh snow. Good thing she'd taken the time to get properly dressed before leaving Kristoff's. Her boots were a necessity tonight, not a fashion accessory. Except for their slick soles.

She slipped a little and grabbed at the car's back bumper, but Seth caught her hand. "I've got you."

A small Bobcat rounded the drive-through and into the main lot, plowing snow ahead of it. The headlights caught her in the eyes, and she winced, holding up her free hand to shield her face from the sudden brightness. The plow trundled past, and Dixie got a glimpse of Dan's familiar form hunched in the cab. She couldn't see much beyond the bulky parka and knitted hat, but it was certainly his nose and chin. Not that he looked her direction for even a split second. He was focused on her job like she wasn't even there.

Dixie shook her hand free of Seth's and took a step toward the Bobcat, but it drove right out of the unplowed lot, down the block, and into the competition's parking lot.

Great. What was she supposed to do now?

"You're sure it was her?" Tony's voice rang with sympathy.

"Uh, yeah. I know Dixie when I see her. Her coat, her red purse." Her blond hair blowing in the cold wind. Her hand blocking the beams of the Cat. Blocking him. Of course, she'd do that, standing hand-in-hand with some guy in a parking lot at three in the morning.

"I thought you said Juanita said—"

"That Dixie had news for me? Probably got engaged to that other guy or something."

"You don't know that, Dan. She took a step toward you."

"Dude. If I'd stopped, I'd have decked that bloke for touching my woman. That would have been a great time to find out she was in love with him, wouldn't it?" Dan paced the living room. He needed to keep his voice down. The kids were still asleep, but it wouldn't be long. Mandy, especially, had taken to waking up early over the school break. It was like she couldn't get enough pictures colored in a day. Her new set of one hundred gel pens would dry out any minute now.

"Pray for her." Tony stood in front of Dan, blocking his path, arms crossed over his chest. "I mean, really pray. Pray for her to meet Jesus. Pray for the best thing for your relationship, long term. Pray for what's best for the kids."

"Tony? Shut up."

"Not happening."

Darkness suffocated Dan's mind. All he could see was Dixie's startled face, then her hand lifting to block him, her other hand clasped in that unknown guy's. He knew Dixie. She wouldn't stay single long. She'd been seen with Basil a few days ago, now this guy.

No wonder she wasn't texting or calling him. She'd already moved on.

His heart splintered in two. "Oh, God," he cried.

Tony guided him to the sofa and pushed him to sitting.

In utter despair, Dan cradled his face between his hands, feeling the hot tears flow. His voice broke. "I believed, Tony. I had complete faith it was just a matter of time until she'd see the hope we have in Jesus. That she'd be attracted to Him."

He heard the nearby armchair creak as Tony lowered himself into it.

"Where did I go wrong? Is it my fault? Is it because I'm not good enough in some way?"

"Man, you *know* you're not good enough."

The words stabbed. He looked up through blurry eyes.

"That's why you needed Jesus," Tony went on.

Somehow, Dan had forgotten. Well, not forgotten exactly, but lost his focus. He drove his hands through his hair. "I feel like I've failed her. That if she'd seen Jesus in me, she'd give her life to Him. Instead, she's rejected Him along with me, and it's my fault."

"It's not your fault."

"It has to be." Everything always was.

"Dan, you're not that powerful."

He shook his head. "I don't know what you mean."

"She's making her own choices, man. You can't make them for her." Tony's voice gentled. "You can pray for her and for Juanita as they meet for counsel. Don't give up praying, but that's all you can do. You have to take your hands off and let God do His thing."

Dan envisioned unwrapping his hands and heart from

around the woman he loved. Could he truly let her go, even if she'd chosen someone else? That meant trusting God more than he trusted himself. And, yeah, the words were easy.

Doing them? Not so much.

20

*H*e should have bought that child-size car for Buddy in the summertime. At this time of year, it required unending snow removal of the expansive back patio to keep the little guy happy. The four-year-old tried to help, but the little toy shovel could barely move a cupful of snow at a time.

Dan leaned on his long-handled shovel and caught his breath. Right now, he wished for a wide back gate on the fenced yard. The Bobcat could clear this space in three minutes flat, but there was no access, not even a man-gate.

"I help, Daddy."

"I know, Buddy." Trying to keep his despair from showing to the kids over the past few days had been a moment-by-moment battle. Mandy had been quieter than usual, taking her gel pens and coloring sheets up to the window seat in the room she shared with her brothers. Henry'd been delighted to discover them, and the walls now sported a mosaic of glittery lines.

An online search told Dan to use hairspray or nail polish

remover. Yeah. That would have been easy if Dixie still lived here.

He missed her like crazy. And, man, keeping the situation in God's hands instead of his was like trying to wrestle an octopus into an open-cab Bobcat. Futile.

"Shovel more snow."

Little dictator. But at least one member of the household was happy, so Dan picked up his shovel and began clearing another section of the patio. In another half hour, he would be done. Or, at least, as done as he could get since it had already begun to snow again. Not only would it be another working night, but he could look forward to coming home and shoveling the patio again in the morning.

Yay.

Finally, he leaned on the long handle and surveyed the handiwork. "Want some hot chocolate, Buddy?"

"No. Drive car now."

Dan shook his head. He'd created a monster with that gift, but there was only an hour before dusk, so the little boy might as well play outside while he could. Dan opened the sliding glass door and stripped off his outdoor gear. He carried everything across to the entry at the front of the house and put it away.

The kids were sure quiet. Henry would awaken from his nap any minute. Dan wouldn't complain about time to put his feet up on the coffee table before the toddler demanded full alert. He should probably make supper, but hadn't Tony said he'd be back in time for that? He was going to miss the other man when he moved out in spring.

Dan poured himself a coffee, zapped it in the microwave, then settled in his recliner with his Bible app open. He'd been derailed from the reading schedule he'd established before winter blew in, but he could do some reading now. He tapped Psalm 147 and began to read.

He heals the broken hearted and binds up their wounds.

Dan closed his eyes. *Please, Lord. Heal me. Bind my wounds.*

Sing to the Lord with thanksgiving. Dan scanned the assorted reasons to be thankful, but his heart knew his big one. Forgiveness. Salvation.

The Lord takes pleasure in those who fear him, in those who hope in his steadfast love. Praise the Lord...

From upstairs came Henry's wail. Dan waited for Mandy's comforting voice for her little brother but heard nothing. With a sigh, he swung the footrest lever down, glanced out to see Buddy in his car, and got to his feet.

He lifted the toddler from his crib, and the sobs immediately stilled as Henry burrowed against his neck. Dan rubbed the little guy's back. "Hey, Daddy's boy. Did you have a good sleep?"

Henry squirmed, his sweaty curls rubbing Dan's jaw while his little fingers flexed on Dan's shoulder.

"Where's your sister?"

No reply, not that Henry was given to many words.

Dan changed the baby's diaper then hoisted him back to his arms. He peeked into the master bedroom and even into Tony's room, where the door stood ajar.

"Mandy?" But she didn't answer. The bathroom door was open, too.

Dan frowned and took a closer look around the second story, but she really wasn't anywhere up there. He took the steps two at a time and scanned the main floor as panic flared within him. Where could she be?

"Mandy! It's not hide-and-seek time. Come out now."

Still nothing. Dan stepped into the backyard. He already knew she wasn't playing with her brother, but he had to look. And, of course, she wasn't there. "Buddy, have you seen Mandy?"

The boy shook his head. "Car go fast. See?" He sped across the patio, nearly quickly enough to pass a tortoise.

"That's great." Dan stepped back into the house and closed the door, clutching the toddler. What had happened to Mandy? She'd been coloring when he'd gone outside to shovel, and there was a clear line of sight between the two doors. Of course, he hadn't been staring at the front door while he'd been working.

He looked in the entryway again. Her boots were gone. Her shiny purple parka was gone. Her ballerina backpack was gone.

Mandy was gone, and it would be dark soon.

His heart seized.

⌒‿‿

"GET DOWNSTAIRS RIGHT THIS MINUTE."

Dixie held her phone away from her ear, stared at it, and put it back. "Hello to you, too, Mom."

"This nonsense has gone on long enough. Get down here."

"Here?"

Mom snorted. "Are you some kind of moron? Yes, I'm outside. We need to talk."

"But—"

There was a shuffling sound then a small voice said, "Mama?"

Dixie's blood ran cold as she sprang off Tanisha's sofa. "Mandy?"

"I love you, Mama. I miss you."

"I love you, too, baby. Put Grandma back on, okay?"

Sniffles. "Okay."

"Are you coming downstairs *now*?" There was a triumphant ring to Mom's voice.

"What have you done?"

"A girl needs her mother, don't you think?"

Had she entirely lost her senses? "Does Dan know where she is?"

Mom laughed. "Dan's got nothing to do with it. He can have the boys."

"Mom, there are legal things going on here. You can't just — what *did* you do, anyway?"

Her mother's voice grew icy like the late December wind. "He said I couldn't see my own granddaughter. That I had to ask some lawyer's permission. Well, I showed him, didn't I?"

This didn't sound good. Dixie grabbed her coat and shoved her arms into the sleeves then yanked up her boots. She headed for the stairs.

"Dixie?"

"Coming, Mom. You stay put. I'll be right down."

"I thought you'd see it my way."

How had Dixie never noticed her mother had shifted beyond eccentric and on to erratic? She clattered down the stairs and pushed through the main apartment doors. Her mother's car idled in the lot and, through the back window, Dixie could make out a small form.

Oh, how she'd missed her daughter! But this wasn't right.

Dixie pulled on the backdoor handle, but it was locked, so she opened the passenger door instead. She knelt on the seat and reached to hug her daughter.

Sobbing, Mandy wrapped her arms around her neck.

"It's okay, baby." Dixie stroked the long tangled locks.

"Grandma yelled at me," Mandy sniffled. "I want Daddy."

Dixie fixed a glare on her mother sitting behind the wheel. "What's going on?"

"No man is going to keep Wayling women apart. We'll show him."

Mom had to be high on something from the slightly crazed look in her eyes. For the first time, fear trickled down Dixie's throat. Not just anger that Mom had apparently snatched Mandy when Dixie had been thinking through how to reunify her family via the proper channels, but actual fear for what an unhinged woman might do.

"Let's drive over to Bridgeview." She tried for a casual tone.

Mom snorted. "Are you kidding me? I was thinking more of Vegas." She shifted the car into gear.

"No way! We're not going that far. I've..." No, Dixie didn't have a job anymore. She couldn't lie about it. "You've got a job. A boyfriend." She forced that last word out as she thought of the creepy guy Mom had been with a few days ago.

"He's gone." Mom veered onto the street, and Dixie's door swung before she pulled it closed.

"We can't just do this. We need clothes, toothbrushes..." Wallets. Dixie's was up in the apartment. All she had was her phone, tucked into her rear jeans pocket. She didn't even have a jacket.

"I've got money. Buckle up." The car sped toward the nearest north-south thoroughfare.

"Mom, no!" But Dixie snapped her seat belt. A quick glance over her shoulder revealed Mandy pulling her buckle around as she sobbed quietly. Of course, her booster was in Dan's truck. "Mom, listen to me."

"No, you listen to me. We've got everything we need, the three of us. Don't need no stupid men."

There was no universe where Dan fit that label. The only stupid thing he'd done was hooking up with Dixie in the first place, but he'd seen something no guy before him had. Somehow, he'd figured Dixie was a diamond in the rough, worthy of respect. Worthy of love. They'd started off on the wrong foot, but that's who they'd been back then. Juanita had told her owning up to her past — repenting of it — was necessary, but she couldn't dwell on the mistakes.

There was no way she could be part of this, whatever had overtaken her mother. Somehow, she needed to get through to her before they reached city limits. If it were only her, she'd take her chance bailing out at a stoplight, but she wouldn't have a chance to get Mandy, too. And, when they hit I-90, it would be that much harder. Not to mention that daylight was quickly fading.

Her phone. But making a call or sending a text without

her mother grabbing for it would be difficult. Did she have any other options?

Think, Dixie, think.

But nothing else came to mind.

It had to be a phone call. Texting would take too long, unless she just tapped in *Call 911*. Would the recipient just do that, or ask what was going on? If it were Dixie on the receiving end, she'd think it was a joke.

Dan would take it seriously. He had to know Mandy was missing by now. In the absence of clues, he'd suspect Dixie.

Her head throbbed, but she couldn't take the time to indulge herself. "Tell me what happened, Mom."

"He thinks he's so smart. So much better than me or you. He deserves this."

"That's no answer. What did you do?"

Her mother kept raving about Dan's ego as she swerved onto North Maple. They'd be crossing the river above Bridgeview in a few minutes, and the interstate was not far beyond.

Dixie took a deep breath and shifted in her seat. Why did she always put her phone in her left hip pocket? That made it doubly hard to get out without Mom seeing her.

Sirens grew louder. Mom cursed as cars pulled off to the side, but she did, too.

Dixie quelled the hope that the sirens were for them. "What's going on?" she asked as she reached around behind herself and tugged her phone free. "Can you see?"

Two police cars flew southbound, sirens screaming.

Mandy's sobs increased in volume.

Mom swiveled in her seat and glared at the little girl.

"Shut up. This is for your best. We Wayling women stick together."

Dixie tapped Dan's name in her texting app. *Call 911.* Send. *Mom...*

Her mother's hand grabbed the phone away. "What do you think you're doing?" She pressed the window controller until a gap appeared.

Dixie tried to snatch the device back, but Mom dropped it out the window as she steered back into traffic. "Grow up, Dixie. Don't be so stupid. And shut that kid up."

"I need to get in the backseat with her then."

"Fine, but I'm not stopping."

Dixie unsnapped her belt and crawled through the narrow gap. Mandy reached for her from the middle seat. Must have been force of habit for her to sit there, since of the three kids, she was the only one able to latch her own buckle. Dixie settled in where she could keep an eye on her mother and wrapped her arms around her daughter.

She'd wanted to see Mandy — and the boys, of course — but not like this. Not basically a kidnapping. They'd have to stop for fuel somewhere, though if Mom had planned this instead of just snapped, they'd be a long way from Spokane before that became a necessity. Same with a pit stop for food or restrooms.

As if on cue, Mandy said, "I have to go potty."

"Hold it," Mom growled. "I'm not stopping." She cranked the radio in an obvious effort to ignore the girl.

Mandy sobbed. "But I have to."

Dixie rubbed her daughter's trembling shoulders, helpless to meet the little girl's need.

The lights of Kendall Yards rolled by outside the

window then land dropped away, and the Spokane River flowed far below as they soared over the bridge. Amid those lights sat the beautiful house she'd once lived in when she'd been too stupid to know how good she had it. Her two small boys were down there, safe from their tyrant of a grandmother.

And Dan. Dan Ranta, the only man who'd ever truly loved her. The only man she'd ever loved. Would she see him again? Have the chance to reconcile? Or was her obviously insane mother going to ruin everything?

This would be a good time to start praying. Juanita had told her God cared about her and would meet her needs if she only trusted. She had a big need right now. Safety for her and her daughter. Especially Mandy.

God? It's me, Dixie. I need help...

21

Friends and neighbors crowded into Dan's living room. All it had taken was one call to Tony, asking if he'd seen Mandy, and word she was missing had gone out to the Santoro clan and, well, everyone.

He'd phoned the police, his mind stuttering that Dixie could have stooped to kidnapping, but what else could he think? Who else would do such a thing?

The policemen had fired a billion questions at him, and he'd answered as best he could in his daze. He'd been in the backyard, shoveling. Yes, she missed her mama. No, she'd never run off before. Yes, she could probably reach the deadbolt if she stretched.

Why, though? That was Dan's big question as the officers called in MUPU, the Missing and Unidentified Persons Unit, to begin a search.

Tony stepped into the ring of officers surrounding Dan. "Basil's in Seattle. He sounded genuinely shocked and said he hadn't seen Dixie since the night of the Christmas concert."

It had been a long shot. Basil Santoro might have a thing for Dixie and a penchant for too much booze, but Dan couldn't imagine him acting criminally against a child.

Outside, darkness had fallen with an accompanying drop in temperature. Snow fell.

A small child like Mandy would need shelter to survive a night like this.

Dan dropped his head and drove his hands through his hair. *Oh, God, please help us find Mandy! Whatever the messes of her parents, she doesn't deserve this.*

His phone buzzed with an incoming text, and he grabbed it up.

Call 911. From Dixie?

The police had already sent someone to her apartment, but Tanisha hadn't seen her since the day before. She pointed out Dixie was probably in the laundry room or visiting a neighbor, though, since her jacket and purse were in their places. Her car was home, too.

He showed his phone to the nearest cop. The guy narrowed his gaze and nodded. "Phone her back."

Dan tapped her number. It rang then went to voice mail. "It's Dan. Call me."

Silence reigned for what seemed like a long time, but nothing happened.

He jerked to his feet and paced to the patio door, where Buddy's little car sat under the overhang while snow blew beyond it. He'd have to shovel again tomorrow. He'd need to plow parking lots tonight.

No. He couldn't. He tapped his dad's number. "Hey, Dad. A bit of an emergency here. Mandy's missing."

He could all but see the frown on his father's face. "She what? It's twenty below and snowing."

"I know." All too well. "Listen, can you drive the Bobcat tonight? I can send you the list of parking lots that are my responsibility. Joe and Dennis have their own lists."

"Yeah. Guess so. But what's with the kid?"

"I don't know. The police are here. They've called in searchers. If you were the praying sort, I'd ask you to pray."

Dad harrumphed. "I'll tell your mother. Need help?"

Wow, unexpected. "Just with the plowing. I've got the Cat parked on the trailer here. I'll let you know if anything changes."

"Do that."

Fran's hand touched his arm. "May I take the boys to my house for the night?"

"I..." Could he let them out of his sight when it seemed Mandy might not have just wandered outside on her own? Someone besides Dixie must have snatched her. But who?

One of the police officers conferred with Fran at Dan's nod, offering an escort. Fran's husband, Tad, was obviously torn between helping with the search and staying with Fran and the children, but the officer convinced him to go home and keep watch.

Dan hugged the two little boys while Fran gathered a few clothes from their room upstairs. Then they drove away as Marietta trudged down the sidewalk.

He held the door for her. "Marietta, you didn't have to come."

"Of course, I did. Antonio says the little girl is missing. I cannot help search, but I can make coffee and sandwiches." She jabbed her finger into the chest of the police officer beside Dan. "You know where my house is. You send people there to warm up and eat, yes?"

"It would be better for this house to be headquarters."

Marietta rolled her eyes. "And how am I to bake cookies in someone else's kitchen? My bread, my cans of tuna, everything is at my house."

The officer's eyes softened. "You want to start cooking, ma'am, go for it. We might haul provisions down here, though. One of the neighbors can see to it."

"Humph."

In any other situation, Dan might have found her expression funny. She obviously wanted to be at the center of everything. He gave her a sideways hug. "Thanks for being so thoughtful."

She looked around. "We have a prayer meeting before I go back home, si?"

"Please."

Jasmine slipped her arm around her nonna. "Then I'll come help you cook." She patted her slightly rounded belly. "The little one would rather I didn't spend the night outside."

Nathan stepped up beside her. "And the little one's father thinks that's a great idea." He turned to Dan. "But I'm in on the search, no matter how long it takes."

"Prayer first," insisted Marietta. She marched into the center of the room and clapped her hands before launching into an impassioned plea to God above for Mandy's safety.

Half of it was in Italian, but Dan got the gist. He choked back tears, barely keeping his emotions in check. He'd be of no help if he fell apart now. Mandy needed him to think clearly. *Please, Lord.*

An officer answered his phone, holding up his hand for silence. Everyone but Marietta obeyed. The man's gaze found Dan across the crowded room, and he jerked his head.

Dan wended his way around the room toward the front entry as hope bubbled. "What is it?"

"A woman driving south on Maple saw a phone drop out of a car window in front of her. She swerved to miss it then stopped to pick it up before someone ran over it. The screen was cracked, but the message app was still visible. The last delivered message said *Call 911*. There was one word on the next line that hadn't been sent. Simply *Mom*." The officer stared hard at Dan. "The phone is in a silver glitter case, and it's registered to Dixie Wayling."

Dixie. He took a deep breath. "That's the text I got, then."

The cop nodded. "Someone's gone to get the phone from the woman who called it in. There might be other clues."

"What kind of car? Gray Buick?"

"Yes. She didn't get a license plate, though. You know the car?"

"Dixie's mother. Eunice Wayling." He rattled off her address and showed her phone number to the cop, who stepped aside and called his superior.

"Gray Buick?" asked Rebekah Roper, who lived down the street. "I've seen a car like that in the neighborhood several times lately. Goes really slow to the other end by Adriana and Myles's, turns around, and comes back."

"Would the child open the door to this woman?" asked the police officer.

Dan closed his eyes and took a deep breath. "She probably would, yes."

The big question was, what would Eunice want with Mandy? And with Dixie...

DIXIE CRADLED Mandy against her side as the little girl relaxed into sleep. The lights of Spokane disappeared in the distance, and swirling snow stabbed through the headlights at the windshield.

Mom was driving too fast for road conditions. The car slid a little here and there, but Dixie couldn't hear her cursing — though she saw the lips move — over the rock music blaring from the radio.

All she could do was pray... and hope for a chance to escape when her mother finally stopped for fuel. Maybe Ritzville. Maybe not until the Tri-Cities.

The panic had subsided. Mostly. Whatever was going on, her mother wouldn't purposefully hurt her or Mandy. Would she? Dixie closed her eyes.

God, it's me again. Dixie. I don't know how to pray, but Juanita says You hear us when we talk to You. I know I'm one of Your newest kids, but I've got kind of a big problem, and I don't know what to do. My mom's gone loony, and she's, uh, kidnapped us.

Her eyes sprang open. Really? Kidnapped? That's what it was called when someone forced others to come with them against their will, wasn't it? That meant her mom was a criminal.

I love my mom. Best to be completely honest with God. *Or, at least, I care about her. And I really love my daughter. I don't want anything bad to happen to her. I don't want her scarred for life. Can I trust You?*

A measure of peace settled over Dixie like a soft downy duvet. Juanita said God was always with her, caring for her, and she could kind of feel it. She stared out into the night, but it didn't seem quite so black.

That prodigal son had faced a deep darkness, too. He'd sensed a light shone somewhere, if he only returned to his father's house. Juanita had told her about a verse — she couldn't remember where — about God calling people out of darkness into His wonderful light.

So, Dixie needed faith. She needed to put her hope in the God she'd met just a few days ago. She needed to let Him prove He was trustworthy.

I'm doing my best to trust You.

"WITH THE PHONE CALL, and with the vehicle matching the description of the child's grandmother's car, we believe there is zero probability the child might be out wandering the neighborhood."

The unspoken consolation — no chance Mandy would be found in the icy river. A teensy tiny part of him still feared that, even though all evidence pointed to Eunice.

"So, we're calling off the ground search. State patrol is watching for a car matching her license plate number and description." The officer turned to Dan. "Any clue where she might be going?"

Dan rubbed his temples. "I couldn't tell you, no. Eunice has lived in Spokane all Dixie's life. I don't remember her talking about friends or family in other places. Mind you, she never had any use for me, so I haven't spent a lot of time with her."

The police officer nodded. "We've alerted Idaho and Oregon, as well as the Canadian border. She's got to stop sometime, and we'll get her then." He touched Dan's shoulder. "Don't worry about your little girl."

The reassuring words wouldn't stop his anxiety. Only God could do that.

A murmur of voices as a few people gathered their coats and went out into the cold night, their services not required after all.

"I phoned Nonna," came Tony's quiet voice. "She seems disappointed no one needs her sandwiches."

Dan managed a grin. "I'm not hungry." His stomach growled. "Or I didn't think I was, but I guess we never had supper."

Nathan chuckled. "I'll go up and get the food. Be back in a few." He headed for the door, shrugging into his coat.

It wasn't even nine o'clock. How could Dan think about eating when he didn't know where Mandy was?

Or Dixie. He let his mind go there for a brief moment. The relief when she'd proved not to be behind the little girl's disappearance had nearly dissolved his knees. Dixie had issues, no doubt about it, but she wouldn't make the same mistake twice. She'd tried to reach him to get help. Thankfully the stranger had rescued the phone from the street instead of driving over it.

Eden, Sadie, and Rebekah left the house, Rebekah with six-month-old Theodore in a baby wrap on her chest. Soon they were down to one police officer and the men from Dan's prayer group.

He looked around, meeting each pair of eyes in turn. Jacob. Wade. Myles. Peter. Alex. Tony. Wesley. Marco. Pastor Tomas. Only Tad and Nathan were missing, each on his own related mission.

Marco spoke. "Time to pray, my brothers." The men draped their arms across each other's shoulders, tightening into a circle, and bowed their heads. "Jesus, we come."

Dan listened as, one after the other, his friends raised his and his family's concerns to the Lord, offering an amen to each other's prayers, and continuing to pray, back and forth across the circle in no discernible pattern.

He was vaguely aware of a place opening for Nathan when he reentered the house, of the officer tapping on his laptop over at the table, but most of him was consumed by the brotherhood these men had freely offered.

Dave Junior had never been at his side the way these neighbors were. Little held them together besides Ranta blood. But, here, in the family of God, he belonged. No matter what happened, how this night played out, Dan knew, beyond a shadow of a doubt, that God would never leave him. He'd sent His ambassadors to surround Dan and lift him up.

22

J wish that guy would stop tailgating me with his high beams on." Mom adjusted her side mirror. "It's an interstate. There's an entire free lane to pass me if he wants to go that fast."

Dixie shifted in the backseat, settling Mandy's head on her lap. She stroked the tangled curls away from her daughter's face. The glare from the vehicle's lights illuminated the car. Mom was right. It was following very closely, and that took some doing since Mom had been flying right along since they'd left Spokane.

Mom tapped the brakes, and the car fishtailed slightly on the snowy pavement.

The guy flashed his lights.

What on earth?

Then a siren screeched, and red and blue lights strobed the darkness.

Mom cursed and stomped on the accelerator.

Dixie's breathing hitched. Memories of the night Basil ran a police block slammed into her, but he'd been driving under the influence. Mom wasn't, at least not that Dixie could tell, but she was definitely being influenced by something. She might not be the sweetest, most loving, mother and grandmother on the planet, but Dixie had never felt afraid of her before.

Dear God, it's me again. Dixie.

Not that she'd really stopped talking to Him for the past couple of hours. She'd been praying for an opportunity to get away from her mother. Whether the police were after her mother for speeding or something else, this would be her best chance. She waved both arms, hoping they'd show in the bright glare of the headlights.

"Stop it, Dixie."

"Mom, pull over. You can't outrun the police."

In reply, Mom sped up and moved to straddle the dotted line as though trying to prevent the car behind them from passing, but it fell back.

Dixie felt fear burgeon again. Why weren't the police forcing Mom off the road? But then she heard a bump-bump as they flashed by a vehicle at the roadside, and Mom wrestled with the steering wheel as the car turned into a sideways skid.

The air blued with Mom's frantic snarls as she struggled to regain control, and Dixie shouted prayers in an attempt to cover the curses, pressing her hand over Mandy's ear and keeping the little girl down.

They were going to crash. Mandy wasn't in a booster. Would the lap belt give her whiplash?

Frenzied thoughts whirled through Dixie's mind in the few seconds before the car slid off into the median, pivoting to face the direction they'd come. Lights and sirens from three police cars filled the air.

Mom growled and pounded the steering wheel then tried to drive out, but between the snow on the ground and what was probably punctured tires from spike strips, the car only slid a few inches to the side.

The driver's door was yanked open and a police officer shone his flashlight in Mom's face. "Eunice Wayling? Out of the car. You are under arrest for kidnapping."

Mandy sat up, tears pouring down her cheeks, and she reached for Dixie.

"Oh, baby." Dixie pressed the little girl to her chest. "Everything will be okay now."

If only she could prevent her daughter from seeing her own grandmother clasped in handcuffs. If only she didn't have to see it herself, but she couldn't turn away.

"I want Dan—" Mandy hiccuped. "I want Daddy."

"I know, baby. Soon." Emotions roiled over Dixie as fear ebbed. Would Dan understand she had nothing to do with this? Would he believe her when she told him she'd prayed with Juanita just a few days ago?

The beam shone into the backseat. "Dixie? Mandy? Are you okay?" The male voice was gentler than the one demanding her mother's exit from the car.

"Yes, sir."

"Let's get you two somewhere safe." He opened the door, and Dixie climbed out, reaching back for Mandy. Her daughter was nearly too heavy to carry, especially up the slippery slope, but Mandy attached herself around Dixie's body and refused to let go. With a police officer assisting from either side, Dixie made it to the nearest car carrying her burden.

Just over from them, Mom was pushed into the backseat of another vehicle, hands behind her back.

Dixie's heart clenched. She wanted to rush over there, assure the cops that her mother was innocent. That she was a loving parent and would never do anything as horrific as kidnap her child and grandchild. But Dixie couldn't do that. It had happened, and her mom had to face the consequences.

The radio crackled as the officer climbed into the driver's seat. "Suspect in custody."

He glanced over his shoulder at Dixie and gave her a lopsided smile as he picked up the handset. "I have Dixie and Mandy Wayling safe. Proceeding to Franklin County's Sheriff's Office for debriefing."

⌐ ⌐

"THEY'RE SAFE IN PASCO." The officer rose from his position at the table then stretched both hands over his head until something cracked.

Dan — all the guys — had heard the report coming through the scanner. They'd taken a break for Marietta's sandwiches then returned to the business of praying. Now they all grinned at each other, the relief in the air palpable.

Dan turned to the officer. "How are they getting home? Can I go get them?"

"You sure, man?" asked Tony quietly.

"That's *my* little girl. She needs me." And then there was Dixie, somehow a victim in all this as well. Yeah, he wanted to see her again, too. He wanted to wring her neck then hug her tight and never let go.

"I'll make a call." The officer turned away. In a minute, he returned with a slip of paper. "You're cleared. Here's the address."

That had to mean Dixie knew he was coming. He had her permission.

"I share Tony's concern." That was Jacob. "If it were just Mandy, I'd understand, but there's Dixie, too. How does that work with the lawsuit and all?"

"Give Sadie a call." Peter held out his phone. "Just run it by her."

Dan stepped back and glared at his friends. "Don't you guys get it? We've been praying for a breakthrough. This might not be how I envisioned it happening, but I'm not sitting here, safe and warm, while my girls go through this without me. My dad's working for me tonight. Fran has the boys. I'm too wired to sleep. There's no reason at all for me not to drive to Pasco."

Wade nodded. "I'm a father. I get it. If something happened to Olivia or Theodore, I couldn't sit tight and wait for their return if I could get to them more quickly. Go in peace, brother. Know we will continue to pray."

"Agreed," said Marco. "Need someone to ride along?"

Dan shook his head. As good as company on the drive down sounded, he needed to have a heart-to-heart with Dixie on the way back. Juanita had said Dixie had news for him. He needed to hear it straight from her, whether she was seriously dating some other guy or something else was going on. But maybe, just maybe, with all that had happened today, she'd be willing to listen to him talk of answered prayer, of how much he still cared for her. Loved her.

Lay it all on the line one more time, come what may.

Dan elbowed past his friends and grabbed his parka from the front closet. Then he stomped into his boots and checked his pocket for his wallet and keys. "Let yourselves out when you're done. Last one, lock up behind you."

He strode out to his truck and unhooked the trailer holding the Bobcat, resting the hitch on a block. Dad could get it from there. Then he drove out into the night. Just him and God.

~ ⌒ ~

MANDY STRADDLED DIXIE'S LAP, the child's arms tight around her mama's neck even as she slept. Dixie wouldn't complain. She'd had far too little of that sort of snuggling in recent months. Much longer, really, since she'd spent most of her daughter's life pushing her away.

No more.

If only she hadn't done irreparable harm to the little girl already. No, she wasn't going down that road again. She clung to the fact that God had forgiven her. It would have to be enough.

She shifted slightly on the awkward plastic chair. It seemed she'd been sitting here forever, but it couldn't have been that long. The officer had taken her statement then asked a thousand questions about her relationship to her mother and to her daughter. The Spokane detachment had called early on to see if she was willing for Dan to meet her here and take her and Mandy home.

Dixie was more than willing, even though the word *home* had little meaning. It meant Tanisha's apartment, at least for now. But home was more than a place where she kept her stuff. It was Dan. He was her home, her anchor, her world.

She heard voices down the corridor. Footsteps. And then Dan entered the room. She struggled to rise with the burden of an almost-six-year-old pressing against her, but Dan reached for the child and lifted her as though she weighed nothing.

"Daddy," murmured Mandy, burrowing against his neck, clinging to him.

"I've got you, baby," Dan whispered back, kissing her hair, stroking her back. "I've got you."

Dixie rose on trembling legs, filling her gaze with this man she loved. He was strong enough to comfort a small child, solid enough to withstand whatever life threw at him. She took a shaky step toward him, desperate to feel the sheltering hold of his arms. "Hey, Dan."

Emotion pooled in his dark eyes, and his stubbled jaw flexed. "Dixie. You okay?"

She nodded. "Ready to go home."

"Let's go then." He stepped aside so she could pass into the corridor ahead of him.

They entered the lobby, and the police officer behind the desk rose and approached them. He shook Dixie's hand. "Take care, Ms. Wayling. SPD will be in touch."

"Thank you." She followed Dan out into the blowing snow, and he held the truck door for her while she climbed in then he settled a clingy Mandy into her booster in the back.

He backed out of the parking spot, still not really looking at Dixie. A few minutes later he merged north-bound onto 395.

Was he intending to keep quiet for two hours? Well, he could listen, then, because Dixie had things to say. She cleared her throat, and he shot her a glance across the dark cab, jaw tense.

"I don't know if you've heard, but I've been seeing Juanita Ramirez for the past month or so."

The brush of his gaze this time was softer. "I heard."

"She was on the list of counselors approved by Washington Law Help. I had to do something when you sent that letter, Dan."

He stared out the windshield as they passed the final lights of Pasco. "I had no choice, Dixie. What you did to Mandy at Thanksgiving..."

"I know. I can't tell you how sorry I am."

A measuring gaze flicked her way.

"I don't know if I'll be able to forgive myself if all this traumatizes her for life. Dan, you have to understand. I've changed. Juanita listened to me. She explained things to me." No change in his expression, but Dixie forged on. "She prayed for me."

"That's good."

He didn't understand.

She opened her mouth to continue, but he held up his hand.

"Listen, Dix. When we met three years ago, I was a selfish punk only looking out for myself."

She remembered that New Year's Eve party hosted by Billie and company. She remembered being swept off her feet by the tall, handsome man with the unruly blond hair. His gaze had been so intense, and she'd reacted to his singular attention. She remembered the passionate night that followed, and how he'd moved in with her and Mandy and Buddy just a few days later. How he'd cared for her, cared for her kids, through thick and thin, until she'd messed everything up.

But he was still talking. "I didn't know how to love anyone more than I loved myself, but I learned. I fell for you, Dixie Dawn. Hopelessly. But you weren't enough. You weren't what I needed deep inside."

"You needed Jesus."

This time he stared at her for so long she feared they'd hit the ditch before he looked back to the road. "Yes. I needed Jesus. I needed forgiveness and hope and light."

"I know."

His hands clenched on the wheel, and his jaw worked as though getting his words out was physically painful. "How could you know?"

"Because that's what Juanita showed me. I prayed with her on Christmas afternoon, Dan. Jesus wiped my sin away and made me new."

He slammed the brakes and veered the truck to the side of the road. Then he turned to her, his eyes gleaming in the glow of the dashboard lights. "You're a Christian?"

She nodded simply.

"Then... Basil. That guy in the parking lot..."

"Would you believe both conversations were about God and Jesus and faith?"

"Don't mess with me about something like this." He choked on the words as he reached for her.

She clasped his hands between hers. "I'm not teasing you. It took a lot for God to get through my hard head. I didn't think I deserved better." She grimaced. "My mom did a number on me since I was a kid, but all that ends today. *Jesus* says I have value. *He* says I'm worth saving."

Dan's knuckles swept down her jaw, leaving a trail of fire in their wake. "You have a lot of value, Dixie Dawn." His words were low, guttural.

And then he leaned just a little closer and captured her lips with his.

Home.

Wherever Dan Ranta was, Dixie Wayling was home.

23

*D*an woke on the sofa the next morning, Mandy burrowed against him, arms still wrapped around his neck. His little girl had refused to let him go when he'd carried her into the house at well past two in the morning. It was still dark now.

He tried to shift, but she was a deadweight. Man, he was stiff. Even so, a smile curled his lips.

Had it really happened? Had Dixie finally found Jesus? He remembered the soft sheen in her eyes, the unaccustomed smile, the wonderment in her words. Dixie wasn't a good liar. Whatever she was thinking always displayed itself to everyone around her. And she'd proven over the past seven months that she wouldn't pretend faith she didn't feel just to keep him. She'd been more than willing to let him go. Let the children go, and keep running her own way.

Dan's heart thrummed. The change was real. God had given them a second chance, and Dan was going to do it right this time. Watching for God's guidance every step of the way. Building a new relationship with Christ at the center. Growing together in faith. Receiving godly counsel together.

Together.

He liked the sound of that word. The hope of it had been gone for far too long, but like a seed in a dried-out desert, it sprang to full-blown life with one sprinkle of rain.

Dan chuckled and kissed Mandy's tangled hair. He rearranged her so he could sit up and lay her back on the cushions without him underneath. She sighed and curled sideways, her lashes flickering against her soft cheeks. His little girl, in all the ways that mattered. She was safe.

Please, dear Lord, erase the memories of yesterday from her tender mind.

Dixie had told him Mandy had sat in the window upstairs, staring out, when she'd seen her grandmother's car. Eunice had beckoned, and Mandy had gone with no hesitation when her grandmother promised to take her to her mama.

The early questions hadn't revealed any sinister motives. Eunice's young boyfriend had hepped her up on drugs and ditched her. She'd snapped. Of course, the investigation would continue for some time.

Dan shuddered as he padded into the kitchen and measured coffee grounds into the filter. Tony had been trying to hook him on Italian-style coffee, but nothing beat a good pot of dark roast. When water began to gurgle through the grounds, he turned to the fridge. A plate of Marietta's sandwiches, covered with plastic wrap, awaited him. That would do. He set it on the table, pulled the pot long enough to pour the first cup, and settled at the table with his Bible app open.

Half an hour later, Tony came quietly down the stairs. He glanced at the sleeping little girl across the open space then poured himself a mug of coffee before joining Dan at the table. "Sleep okay?"

Dan managed to keep his chuckle hushed. "Not really. My mind was pretty wired, and that kid weighs more than you'd think."

"I bet." Tony grinned, reached for a sandwich, and poked his chin toward Dan's phone. "Glad to see you're in the Word this morning."

"I need it more than ever."

"How so?"

"The past few months have been like a long, dark tunnel with no exits. I haven't had a lot of choices. Stay the course, or crawl back the way I came, giving everything up."

Tony nodded.

"By the grace of God, I kept moving forward. It was hard. You know it."

"I know it."

"Now..." Dan hesitated, staring out the patio door to where a hint of dawn added shadows to the back yard. "Now it seems like there are choices. Options. It's like coming out of that tunnel into an open field. I could go in any direction, I guess. I know where I want to go..."

Tony chuckled.

"But I need to know for sure. God kept me going in that tunnel. Kept whispering truth to me. I don't ever want to lose that."

"You keep asking, and He'll keep guiding."

"Yeah. Part of me says to go down to City Hall this

morning, apply for a marriage license, and have a wedding in like three days."

"And the other part of you?"

"Says that's jumping ahead of God." Dan shook his head. "Doesn't keep me from wanting it."

"I hear you."

"What do you think I should do?"

Tony's eyebrows rose. "It doesn't matter what I think. You're my friend — my brother — and I'll still be that either way."

"We talked about our future a bit last night. What it might look like. Dixie quit her job at Kristoff's a couple of days ago. She's looking for something else. I just want to swoop in and invite her home, but I held my tongue. We need a little time. I know it, but I want to fix everything ASAP. It's in my nature, I guess."

"It's not a bad trait."

Dan quirked his eyebrows at Tony. "But?"

"But you can't grow her. She has to get in the Word and do that herself."

"Yeah." Dan stared out the glass doors for a moment. The sun still wasn't visible — it didn't shine this deep in the north-facing valley until much later in the morning — but its effects illuminated the snow-covered backyard. "But now I get to court her the way I should have three years ago. Take her out. Sit beside her in church. Have family days." He turned to Tony. "How long will I have to do it that way?"

Tony grinned. He rose, locked his hands together, and stretched above his head. "You'll know."

Over on the sofa, a little girl, tousled from sleep, sat up. "Daddy? Where's Mama?"

Dan held out his arms, and Mandy scrambled over and climbed into his lap. "Remember we dropped her off at Tanisha's last night?"

She nodded, a little frown on her face.

He kissed her hair. "Don't worry. We'll see her today. We'll see her lots of days."

"That's good." She nestled against his chest. "I miss her."

"Me, too, baby. Me, too."

DIXIE ADMIRED herself in the mirror. She was almost ready for their Valentine's Day date with fresh highlights in her hair and a careful application of makeup. A pair of silvery hoops dangled from her ears and caught the light as she twisted one way, then the other. The shimmery dress was just short enough to be sexy while being a good ten inches longer than her Kristoff's uniform.

She wrinkled her nose. There was nothing sexy about her new uniform, white coveralls. Dino Santoro had hired her to help paint the new restaurant as his crew finished the renovation to the building not far from Bridgeview Bakery and Bistro.

Antonio's wasn't open yet. Not for a few more weeks, so that wasn't where Dan was taking her. Just as well, since Tony was putting the kids to bed tonight. She'd met Tony a bunch of times in the past six weeks, and she totally trusted her kids with him.

Dixie sighed. Like she was anyone to talk, but still.

Bzzzt.

The downstairs door, but it was too early for Dan. Her heart skipped a beat all the same.

"I've got it," called Tanisha. A moment later, she stood in the bathroom doorway hidden behind a bouquet of red roses. "Girrrrrrl. That guy is such a keeper."

Dixie swallowed hard, the air filled with sweet perfume. Dan had sent flowers every single week, starting on New Year's Eve to commemorate their meeting three years before. That bouquet had been a bright, playful bunch of gerbera daisies. They'd cheered her heart and given her hope.

But twelve red roses. That was a whole new level. True love.

"That's not all," said Tanisha.

Dixie blinked and took the bouquet from her host then followed her into the living room, inhaling the sweetness. She spotted a small box with a clear plastic lid containing a wrist corsage with a single red rose and a tiny bud.

"Great look with that silver dress. Tonight's the night, hon." Tanisha offered a sideways smile. "I don't mind telling you I'm a wee bit jealous."

Dixie lifted the wristlet from its box and slid it on. "Jealous?"

"Not of Dan, exactly, but the way he's treating you. I didn't think it would look like this."

"I didn't, either." She carried the bouquet into the kitchen and arranged the roses in an antique vase she'd found at a thrift shop. She'd needed two, since the flowers still thrived when the next installment arrived.

"What's it like, being treasured?"

Dixie turned to her friend. "I can't describe it. I've loved Dan for so long, but a lot of the time it was just for how he made me feel, you know? Now I'm seeing him for who *he* is. Thoughtful. Kind. A great daddy."

"And a guy who makes your toes curl."

Dixie grinned. "Oh, yeah."

"And yet you're not sleeping together."

Now *that* had been a struggle at times. "We're, um, learning other ways to communicate."

Tanisha laughed. "I guess that's good, though sex is a powerful language."

"It will come again." Dixie fingered a soft red petal and glanced back at her friend. "We're doing things the right way this time."

"Because of that Jesus thing."

"He's real, Tanisha. I can't even begin to describe it." Although, she'd tried a few times. Her friend deserved that much.

"You don't have to. I can see the difference all over you, and it's not just that you're not coming to the drinking parties. You're... softer, somehow."

"It's all Jesus." With a side order of Dan.

Tanisha gave a wistful sigh then straightened as the buzzer rang again. "There's your date. Have fun. Tell me all about it when you get home."

"You're not going out tonight?"

Tanisha wrinkled her nose. "Nah. There's no one special enough for Valentine's Day this year, and I don't feel like a drink just for drinking's sake. You know?"

Dixie gave her an impulsive hug before reaching for her coat. "I'll see you later, then."

THE ATMOSPHERE inside Wild Sage Bistro was all Dan had hoped for when he'd made the reservation weeks before. Sparkling lights festooned the windows along with the draperies, and a flickering candle sat on every wooden table. The hostess led them to a place against the wall, and Dan slipped Dixie's faux fur coat from her shoulders and draped it over the leather club chair.

She was stunning in that shimmery dress. Her eyes sparkled in the candlelight as she thanked him.

Dan kissed her. Just a peck, because he couldn't help himself. "You're beautiful, Dixie Dawn," he whispered.

She sank into her seat as he pushed it in then he rounded the table, hung his leather jacket over the spare chair, and took his own seat. He reached across the table and gathered her hands, lightly skimming the rose at her wrist.

"Can I get you something to drink?" asked the waiter.

Dan tore his gaze from their entwined hands. "Uh. Do you want something, babe?"

"I better not. Unless there's something nonalcoholic?"

His heart swelled at the change in her as the waiter rattled off several options.

"The pomegranate ginger spritzer sounds good."

"Make that two," he agreed.

He managed to keep his hands off hers long enough to examine the menu and place their order, but then they were there, clasped in the middle again. He ran his thumb over her tapered fingernails. "Dixie, I love you."

She smiled at him. "I love you, too."

It wasn't the first time they'd shared those words in the past six weeks or even in the past three years. They meant something now, more than they had. Dan's heart was full of wonder as their gazes met and clung. They'd weathered so much, come through so strong.

He leaned a few inches closer, gaze intent. "Dixie, will you marry me?"

Dan hadn't meant to do it this way. He'd meant to get on one knee and all that. Maybe it wasn't too late.

Her lips parted, her eyes shining.

He dug in his pocket and moved around beside her chair, dropping to one knee and opening the little box. "Please don't say no again, Dix," he whispered. "I couldn't bear it."

She leaned over and held his face between both her hands before brushing his lips with her own.

The sweet intensity of that brief caress nearly dissolved him, but it wasn't an answer. Not quite.

"I'll marry you tomorrow, Daniel John Ranta."

His breath escaped as he plucked the diamond from its satin nest and slipped it on her waiting finger. "I love you, Dixie." He dropped a sweet kiss to her lips before rising to his feet. "So, so much." He took his seat.

She angled her hand in the candlelight, the gleam playing off the diamond. "Is tomorrow too soon?" She glanced his way, and he could see the vulnerability on her face.

"There's a three-day waiting period in Washington

State." His thumb touched the diamond. "But, babe? Much as I want to make you my own, I think we need to wait a little longer."

Dixie's eyes glistened when she looked over at him. "Longer?"

"I feel you, babe. I do. But I want you to have a real wedding. A pretty white dress. A..."

"I don't deserve the white dress, Dan. You know I don't."

"Sweetheart, did Jesus make you new?"

Hope caught in her eyes. "He did."

"Then you *are* new. Wear white, babe. Wear it knowing Jesus covered everything."

She studied him. "How about Easter?"

Another six weeks. "Sounds perfect."

"Only..." Dixie bit her lip. "Ava asked me to join the church dance troupe for Easter Sunday. She and Fran figured the Christmas one went so well, and there are some kid parts, too."

"Christmas was amazing. Do it. We can have the wedding Sunday afternoon or maybe evening."

"I'd be dancing with Alex if I say yes." She peeked at him. "Is that a bad idea?"

"If you're worried about me being jealous? I'm not." He leaned closer and lifted her chin, so her gaze caught on his. "I trust you totally. And I want you to follow your dreams. I know you've always wanted to dance like that. Would Mandy get a part?"

Dixie nodded, her eyes fixed on his. "She's got a lot of talent for a little kid. Ava wants her. I think doing this production together would be good for our relationship."

"Then do it." His hand grazed her cheek. "It will be a busy weekend, but Linnea and Logan will be home from Edmonds by then, and I can leave the business in their hands for a week or two. We can get away for a honeymoon."

"How about the kids?"

He leaned back in mock horror. "We're not taking them!"

"Silly." She giggled. "That's a long time to leave them with someone."

"Between Tony and Fran and other neighbors, I think we're okay." He tapped her nose. "Let me worry about that. You focus on the Easter performance and the wedding. Keep it simple."

Their plates had arrived, and Dan was suddenly starving. Maybe proposing first had been a good idea, after all.

24

*I*t was interesting how marriage counseling had turned into two families enjoying spending time together. Dixie would never have thought it possible that December day when she'd first entered Juanita's office in fear and trembling.

Now she and Dan ushered their three through the door into the Ramirez house. Nine-year-old Sabrina beckoned Mandy into a world of glitter gel pens and ballerina paper dolls, while six-year-old Emmanuel pulled Buddy through to the trampoline in the backyard. Isaac shared cars with Henry, who was a year younger.

It was a pleasant day for mid-March, and Juanita prepped salads in the kitchen. Dixie rolled up her sleeves to help.

"How are wedding plans coming?" Tomas asked, stirring sugar into a gallon jar of iced tea.

Dixie sent a mock-glare at Dan. "Good, but *he* won't tell me where we're going on our honeymoon. Other than I don't need a passport."

He grinned and shrugged, obviously unrepentant. "You'll find out soon enough."

"I watched a few minutes of the drama practice this week when I was over at the church," Juanita put in. "Wow, I can't believe how professional you guys are. I didn't think you'd ever had lessons before?"

"I didn't, but Ava gets the best out of us all. She's a talented teacher, and we've been working super hard."

"Good for you! And who knew Alex and Evan had that kind of rhythm in them? Even Manny looks pretty good for a little kid."

Dixie laughed. "Your son is naturally dramatic."

"Isn't he, though?" Tomas said wryly. "But I was curious if you two had room for one more big thing Easter weekend."

Dixie frowned over her shoulder at the pastor. Dan leaned against the doorway, arms folded across his chest. It didn't look like this was a surprise to him. "What's that?" she asked cautiously.

"Sadie Guthrie dropped in to see me in the office a few days ago."

Dixie's blood chilled. Dan's attorney. She thought they'd called off the custody hearing completely. She kept her voice even. "Oh?"

"I don't know how well you know her—"

She laughed, a forced sound even to herself.

Dan's arms slipped around her. "Babe, it's not about the kids. Not at all."

"Oh, man. I never thought of that." Tomas's face reddened. "I'm so sorry."

Juanita shook her head. "Men. Tell her what it *is*, not what it isn't."

Now there was some good advice, but Dixie already felt a little reassured in Dan's firm grip. She leaned back against him, eyebrows raised at the pastor.

"Sadie asked if we had a baptism planned for anytime soon. She's been a Jesus-follower for quite a while, but she's never taken that step. I can't think of a better day of the year to host a service like that than Resurrection Sunday." Tomas glanced at Dan then refocused on her. "I talked to Dan for a few minutes after men's breakfast this week, but I want to ask you, too. Are you ready to follow our Lord in baptism?"

Juanita had mentioned the concept in one of their recent counseling sessions, but it had been more on an abstract basis than concrete. Being immersed in the baptism tank represented dying to oneself and rising again, a new creature in Jesus.

Dixie straightened out of Dan's arms and took a few steps closer to Pastor Tomas. "Do you think I'm ready?"

His eyes crinkled with his smile. "New believers in New Testament times were often baptized within minutes of confessing their faith in Jesus. It's not whether *I* think you're ready, but if *you* feel ready to make a public confession of faith."

She lifted both shoulders in a shrug. "Totally. The old me is gone." A sudden thought struck her. "That'd be cool, actually. I was planning to invite Tanisha and Billie and Jared to the drama presentation. I'd like them there when I get baptized, too."

Dan took her hand. "Busy day for them, too, since they'll be back for the wedding at four."

Dixie turned to him. "Are you doing it?"

He nodded. "Absolutely. It's okay if you choose to wait... but I'm glad you'll be right there beside me."

She stretched to press a kiss to his lips. "Beside you all the way, babe."

Dan brushed her cheek with his knuckles. "I like the sound of that." Then he bent to kiss her.

A kiss that took her knees out right there in the pastor's kitchen. She'd all but forgotten their location until she heard Tomas chuckle. Cheeks blazing, she pushed away from Dan.

He laughed, too, love shining from his gorgeous eyes as he winked at her.

That man. She looked over at Juanita. "Um, where were we? Do you need that salad mixed?"

Juanita grinned. "What I need is for Tomas to fire up the grill and start cooking burgers for the troops. Everything in here is pretty much ready."

Tomas held up both hands. "I know when I've been delegated." He jerked his head toward the patio door, beyond which the laughter of two jumping little boys rang out. "Join me?" he asked Dan.

Dan offered Dixie one more lingering smile and hand squeeze before following Tomas outside.

Dixie fanned her face. "Whoa. That man."

Juanita burst out laughing. "Now that's good to see."

DAN SAT beside his mother in the hushed, darkened sanctuary on Easter Sunday morning with Linnea then Logan on the other side of her. If she'd ever stepped in a church for anything but a wedding or a funeral, he didn't know when. As music swelled behind the closed theater curtains at the front, Buddy stood between Dan's knees, peering between the people in the row in front of them. Henry seemed to enjoy the fact that his daddy's knee wouldn't stop jiggling.

The curtains pulled apart as a spotlight brightened on the adult drama team, all on the floor except for Evan Santoro, who opened the performance by 'awakening' the others to the words of *So Will I*.

Dan knew there were other dancers onstage, but once Dixie erupted into her first jump, he had eyes for no one else. The song spoke of God speaking creation into existence, and the human heart's response of worshiping just as creation did. Dan's heart rang with the victorious refrain. *So Will I*. Then the lyrics moved into God's passionate love for His creation, and the beautiful response. Somewhere in there, Mandy and three other kids joined the four men and four women onstage and danced their way to the finale.

Dan's throat choked at the beauty of his gorgeous woman and precious daughter expressing love for the God of the universe. The song spoke of choosing glad surrender, the same way Jesus chose to submit on the cross, knowing that the triumph was coming.

The lights slowly dimmed over the dancers as they held their final positions. The curtains moved back across the stage, and a small light illuminated Tomas at a podium to the side.

"'In the beginning was the Word,'" the pastor quoted

quietly. "'And the Word was with God, and the Word *was* God. He was in the beginning with God. All things were made through him, and without him was not anything made that was made.'"

The spotlight steadily brightened, and Tomas's voice rang out with conviction. "'In him was life, and the life was the light of men. The light shines in the darkness, and the darkness has not overcome it.'"

Tomas leaned on the podium. "Friends, we've just seen a powerful reimagining of creation, but the reality, in the words of the song, was a hundred billion times more dramatic."

Light laughter rippled across the audience. Dixie slipped in beside Dan, and he slid his arm around her shoulder, tugging her close. "Good job, babe." Nearby, Mandy climbed onto Linnea's lap.

"Think of it," Tomas went on. "Think of the One who created everything. The galaxies, the planets, the stars, all of nature. Think of the majesty. Think of the celebration! John chapter one goes on to say, 'The true light, which gives light to everyone, was coming into the world. He was in the world, and the world was made through him, yet the world did not know him. He came to his own, and his own people did not receive him.'"

The place was solemnly quiet as Tomas paused, his gaze scanning the room. "Do you think God didn't know that would happen? That this great gift would be rejected by many? He knew, my friends. He knew. The One who was light itself was abandoned to die in darkness, but it was for a purpose. He allowed His light to be extinguished, but it was temporary!

"Let me read a little more. John says, 'But to all who did receive him, who believed in his name, he gave the right to become children of God, who were born, not of blood nor of the will of the flesh nor of the will of man, but of God.' Today we're going to celebrate with several of our friends and neighbors as they publicly declare their allegiance to Jesus. Because here's the thing, my friends. On Good Friday, we looked into what the death of Jesus means for each one of us."

Dan remembered the evening service a few days back. It had been a powerful reminder of the depth of despair as darkness overtook the known world. He'd felt the crush in his spirit, even though he *knew*, like the early church had not known, how the story would end.

"But without the resurrection, Jesus' death on the cross would have been just one more would-be messiah failing in his mission. It's *because* He rose again that the darkness was pushed back, ushering in a new dawn. It's *because* He rose again, we have new life. It's *because* He rose again that we can celebrate!"

Dixie squeezed his leg. It was time. He passed Henry to Tony, who was sitting behind them, and rose to follow Dixie out of the pew and out the side exit as Tomas wrapped up his brief message.

Sadie soon joined them in the ready room, dabbing tears from her eyes. She reached for Dixie and gave her a big hug. "Thank you. That drama — dance — whatever — was so powerful. I'm so glad you used your talents today."

Dixie hugged back. "Thank you."

From out in the main auditorium someone began to play

the same song on the piano. Dan tilted his head and smiled. Sounded like his brother-in-law, Logan.

Juanita came in. "Everyone ready?"

They all nodded.

"All right, just as we rehearsed, Sadie, you're first. Okay?"

The attorney nodded and stepped into the doorway, waiting for Tomas to call her name. Dan listened as she answered the pastor's questions, affirming her faith, then the big splash and slosh as he dipped her under the water and back up. She accepted a towel from her fiancé's mother and made her way back to the ready room, a big smile on her face.

"Dixie?" questioned Juanita.

His girl nodded, firmly stepping through the door and down the steps into the tank. She stood waist-deep in water, chin up, looking out into the audience where several friends from their old crowd watched.

"Dixie Dawn Wayling," said Pastor Tomas from beside her. "Do you believe that Jesus is the Son of God, who died for your sin and, on the third day, rose again from the dead for the forgiveness of your sins?"

Her voice rang out. "I do."

In just a few short hours, she'd be saying those words to Dan, pledging herself to him in marriage. This day would be nothing short of amazing from one end to the other, a day he'd never seen coming. *Thank You, Jesus.*

"Dixie, I baptize you in the name of the Father, the Son, and the Holy Spirit." Tomas dunked her under the water.

She came up glowing, and Fran was right there to wrap

her in a towel and hug her. She came toward Dan, her face radiant.

He opened his arms, and she walked in, every soaking wet inch of her. It didn't matter if he was half wet when he stepped into the tank himself. This was Dixie's moment. Their moment to share together, like the long, dark night had ended, and daybreak had finally arrived.

25

*D*ixie stood just out of sight at the back of Bridgeview Bible Church, her bouquet trembling, as Ava completed her walk to the front. Mandy grabbed Buddy's hand and hissed at him to behave as she towed him forward. Instantly her face brightened like angelic sunshine as she tossed yellow petals to the carpeted runner. Buddy trudged beside her, carefully holding his pillow level as though a brimming cup of water rested on it. No way was her boy dumping rings off that pillow.

Logan used the entire keyboard on the grand piano as he changed from *So Will I* to the traditional wedding march. People rose and turned toward the back. Lots of people, including Linnea, arm circled around Henry as he stood on the front bench. Dixie had wanted a small wedding, but who could they leave out when the entire community of Bridgeview wanted to celebrate with them?

This was beyond her wildest dream. Even as a teen she'd never expected to be garbed in white, marrying in a church.

She'd never dreamed of a man like Daniel Ranta waiting for her at the altar.

Dan.

Suddenly the qualms left her. It didn't matter that she had no father to walk her down the aisle. That her mother had been court-ordered to stay away from her and the children and thus wasn't present.

All that mattered was her beloved. He'd chosen her. He loved her. And now he waited for her, standing tall between Tony and Pastor Tomas, a look of adoration on his face as he watched her first few hesitant steps toward him.

Buddy grabbed Dan's leg, and Dan bent to pick the boy up. Then somehow Henry kicked free of Linnea and bolted forward. Their friends laughed a little as Dan scooped the almost-two-year-old into his other arm.

From beside Ava, Mandy parked her fists on her hips and scowled before coming to a decision. She dashed across the stage and collided with Dan's side beneath Henry's black leather shoe. Dan grinned down at her, puckering his lips in a mock kiss. He had no hands free for Mandy.

Dixie closed her eyes for a second and took another measured step. This was not how it was supposed to go. Her kids were supposed to stay in their assigned spots, but instead, all three seemed attached to Dan like glue.

But wasn't that how it had always been? From the very first, he'd stepped into a daddy role with Mandy and Buddy, and they'd responded by adoring him. This was her family. She quickened her step — who cared what the tempo of the music dictated?

But Logan must be more observant than that, because the beat sped even as Dixie pushed decorum out of her thoughts. She ran the last half of the aisle then wrapped her arms around Dan and both boys. She gave them a spin before bending to squeeze Mandy.

"Mama hold." Henry reached for her, and she gladly took him.

Logan spun the last bit of the bridal march into some kind of triumphant celebration, and the titters in the audience deepened into chuckles then outright laughter.

They weren't laughing *at* her or the kids, Dixie knew. Their friends were rejoicing *with* them in a wedding no one would soon forget.

Pastor Tomas never quite managed to get the grin off his face throughout his brief words. His eyes twinkled as he coached them through their vows and snickered along with everyone else at Buddy's indignation when Tony produced rings from his pockets. How *could* the rings on his pillow be fake!

All three kids crowded around to admire the rings, and then Pastor Tomas sobered enough to pray a blessing over this new family. "It is my pleasure to introduce to all of you, for the first time, Daniel and Dixie Ranta! Dan, you may kiss your bride."

Dixie's gaze met Dan's, and the grasping of small fingers at her full skirts faded away. As his hands slid around her waist, she stretched hers over his broad shoulders, dug her fingers into his well-gelled hair, and pulled his mouth down to hers.

Finally together. A real family at last.

DEAR READER...

Thanks for reading *Dancing at Daybreak*! I'm so honored that you chose to spend the last few hours with Dixie, Dan, and me. You are appreciated.

I'm an independent author who relies on my readers to help spread the word about stories you enjoy. Would you take a few minutes to let your friends know? Facebook, Twitter, Goodreads... wherever you hang out online.

Also, each honest review at online retailers means a lot to me and helps other readers know if this is a book they might enjoy. I'd sure appreciate your help getting word out.

I welcome contact from readers. At my website, you can contact me via email, read my blog, and find me on social media. You can also sign up for my newsletter to be notified of new releases, contests, special deals, and more! You'll receive *Promise of Peppermint*, the novella that introduces Bridgeview — Rebekah and Wade's story — absolutely free as my thank you gift!

Keep reading for a sneak peek of the next Urban Farm

Fresh Romance book, *Glimpses of Gossamer* (Morley and Alex's story). Enjoy!

- Valerie Comer

www.valeriecomer.com

http://valeriecomer.com/subscribe

Glimpses of Gossamer

— An Urban Farm Fresh Romance 8 —

VALERIE COMER

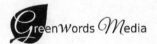

CHAPTER 1

Glimpses of Gossamer
An Urban Farm Fresh Romance 8

a truck engine cut out in Marley Montgomery's driveway. She peeked out the window and inhaled a sharp breath.

A logo on the white truck read SCRAPS, with the words Spokane County Regional Animal Protection Service surrounding it. Oh, no. What was animal control doing here? She had a mighty good guess, and there wouldn't be any evidence by the time the officer finished gathering her things, exited the truck, and rang the doorbell.

Marley dashed out the backdoor into the wildflower-infested yard. Chickens. Where were the chickens? She had too many for the city's bylaws, but she hadn't been able to resist the adorable Silkies. She hadn't been able to bear the responsibility of parting any of them from their friends.

At least the hens had friends. Marley didn't. Not anymore. But she'd make new ones here in Bridgeview, if only she didn't run afoul of the laws. She took a swipe at Bianca and tossed her over the nearest fence. She'd figure out how to get her back later, hopefully before the homeowner returned. Chloe followed, then Deirdre. She just needed to find two more. Any two.

The front doorbell chimed, the sound barely audible through the house.

She had mere seconds left. Where was Gloria? The Buff Orpington loved the deep shade in the far corner, close to the fence. Marley reached into the spot behind the compost bin, felt fluffy feathers, and snagged the bird. She pivoted and let Gloria fly.

"Good afternoon!"

Marley wiped her hands down her ragged jeans and eyed the uninvited — and unwanted — visitor who stepped into view beyond the chain-link fence at the opposite corner of the house. Hopefully she hadn't seen that little maneuver.

The woman was around her own age with red-gold hair in a long braid over one shoulder. A duty belt emphasized her uniform with its spray can and a radio. If she wore a gun, it wasn't visible.

"Hi." Marley approached the gate, pushing her guilty conscience aside and managing a smile.

"Hi. I'm Eden Riehl, and I work for Spokane County Regional Animal Protection Service." The woman touched the logo on her dark blue shirt. "I'm here to investigate a grievance that this property is housing more poultry than zoning allows."

"I'm sorry to hear there's been a complaint." Marley kept the smile in place. Which neighbor? The old man on the east, or the houseful of apparently single men on the west? She needed to start offering free eggs to both sides now that the hens had settled in and were laying again. Only now it would look like bribery.

The officer angled her head and raised her eyebrows. "Are you?"

Marley blinked. "Am I what?"

Ms. Riehl sighed, pulled out a digital pad, and tapped the screen, which she scanned. "This city lot is fifty feet wide and one hundred feet deep, which makes it five thousand square feet. Regulations stipulate you may house up to five chickens *or* two small livestock *or* one small livestock and two chickens." She tapped her stylus and eyed Marley. "How many chickens live on this property?"

"Um..." Marley's mind raced. Honesty might be the best policy, generally speaking, but what was she supposed to do with her extras? Her stepdad would have laughed and said, 'soup pot,' but a girl didn't eat her friends. "I thought the property was longer." She waved up steep hillside behind the house. "The pegs are way up there somewhere. Surely it's bigger than you said."

"How much bigger do you think it is?" The officer's shaped eyebrows angled upward.

Marley wasn't admitting anything. "I, um, thought it was quite a lot bigger."

"Ms... I'm sorry. I don't believe I got your name."

"Marley Montgomery."

"Ms. Montgomery, it's your duty to learn the local laws for animal husbandry, the specific regulations for your particular lot and neighborhood, and then follow them."

Hard to argue with that. She nodded cautiously.

"Are you the homeowner here or a renter?"

"In transition." Marley swallowed hard, tears welling in her eyes. "Gram Renton is still the owner, but she's in a nursing home now with advanced Alzheimer's."

The officer's stance softened. "I'm sorry to hear that. Do the chickens in question belong to Mrs. Renton?"

Marley stared at her bare toe poking at the too-long grass. "No."

"I hope you understand I need to investigate the complaint. May I enter the yard?"

Zephyr was often hidden in a back corner, and only two or three were likely to rush to Marley's side. After her little cleanup operation, she was only one bird over. It would probably be okay. She nodded and shifted away from the gate.

Ms. Riehl stepped through it and looked around. "Wow, you've got a lot going on here."

"No one has cared for the yard in several years, so it's a bit overgrown." A bit. Now *that* was an understatement, but Marley loved the crazy wildness of it. She and Gram Renton would have gotten along great if they'd ever had the opportunity.

"I see that. I never met the previous owner." Ms. Riehl moved down the overgrown path, peering under bushes.

That was an odd comment. Spokane was a city of several hundred thousand people. Most residents never met. Unless the animal control officer meant no one had ever complained about the owner before. Figured Marley'd be the one to get this address registered in the complaint book.

"Oh, she's sweet." Ms. Riehl bent and patted Bella. "I

have a Silkie who looks a lot like her. And she loves attention just as much."

Huh. What was the appropriate response? Marley couldn't think of one.

The officer glanced over at her, but then her gaze went beyond, turning quizzical. She straightened, all her attention now focused on the yard next door.

Marley pinned her smile in place.

"Since when do Alex and Peter have chickens?" The woman muttered as she strode over to the fence, hands on her hips.

Uh oh. Marley swallowed hard. *Be sure your sins will find you out.* That was definitely somewhere in the Bible, and the truth may have just caught up with her.

The officer plucked a black feather off the top of the chain-link fence and turned to Marley, eyebrows raised. "Would you happen to know anything about this?"

In the yard next door, Deirdre fluffed her feathers with gusto in a raised garden bed amid tidy rows of bush beans. Marley held in her gasp. She needed to get her hens back in her own yard before they did any irreparable damage. It was always best to be on good terms with the neighbors.

"Ms. Montgomery?" The woman's voice turned chilly.

"I, um..."

"Are those your birds?"

Marley squeezed her eyes shut then met the officer's gaze. She was so, so sunk. "Maybe? Yes?"

Ms. Riehl's lips tightened. "I suggest you catch them and return them home, and then we'll discuss your infraction."

Not good. Why, oh why had she thought the city bylaws

were more like suggestions? Thought no one would care if she was a couple of birds over? They were sweethearts, and they'd been raised as chicks together. She hadn't had the heart to separate them. Didn't girls need each other?

Not that Marley knew for sure, since she'd been on her own most of her life. But *if* she'd had the chance to be part of a flock like her hens, she'd have been devastated to be separated from them.

Marley caught sight of Ms. Riehl striding for the gate. Better follow. Better obey. She wasn't cut out to be a rebel. Not really.

ALEX SANTORO PEDALED his commuter bicycle up the steep incline into his carport and swung off. He removed his briefcase from the rear rack before lifting the bike to its hooks under the rafters. Then he picked up the briefcase and headed for the back steps, unclipping his bike helmet as he went.

The squawk of a chicken and a flurry of activity assailed him. What on earth? Eden Riehl grabbed for the legs of a white and black bird, who flapped her wings and sidled away. The new next-door neighbor, whom Alex had seen a few times in her backyard, picked up another one and tossed it over the fence. There were at least two other chickens loose in his yard.

Was there a hole somewhere? But then why was Eden here, in uniform? He'd seen her work truck parked in the drive next door but hadn't thought anything of it.

The garden bed nearest the fence was a shambles with

uprooted plants and mounds of black earth where it had been flat, smooth, and weed-free this morning. A model garden.

No more.

Alex set his gear on the bottom step. "What's going on here?" he demanded.

Eden and the other woman straightened, pivoting toward him.

Alex skewered the new neighbor with his gaze then slowly raised his eyebrows.

"Hi." She swept her long blond tangles away from her face, revealing a pretty face, younger than he'd assumed.

But wide-eyed innocence wasn't going to cut it. Not when her fowl created havoc in the gardens he and his family depended on for their business, Bridgeview Backyards. Well, mostly his cousin Peter, since Alex had kept his day job in an air-conditioned office, while their other partner, Alex's sister, Jasmine, was due to have her first baby any day now. The fledgling business had hired a couple of teenage boys to help Peter through the coming busy summer.

The woman still stared at him while the hen that had escaped Eden flapped toward the house.

Alex shook his head and reached for the bird. He caught it easily, dangling it upside down from his hand. "Eden? What do you want me to do with this?"

Eden speared a nasty look at the still-unnamed woman. "I'll take her to one of the truck kennels." She snatched the bird out of his hand and headed to the carport.

"No, please!" The other woman's gaze toggled between

Alex and Eden. "You can't take Bianca. She's been with her sisters all her life."

Bianca?

Eden's lips tightened as she shook her head slightly and continued on her way.

The other woman ran after her, tears flowing down her cheeks.

Alex stepped in front of her. "Who are you, and what is going on here?" She tried to dodge past him, but he shifted sideways. "You're on my property. I think the least you can do is explain."

She turned imploring eyes toward him. "But... Bianca!"

"Who. Are. You?"

She gathered her long hair over her shoulder then her gaze ricocheted off his. "Marley. Marley Montgomery." She thumbed to the ramshackle house on the east side of Alex's. "I moved in there a few days ago."

"Are you a relative of Gram Renton's?"

Her eyes dropped, and her bare toe scuffed in his freshly mown grass. "Sort of?"

"How can you be sort of related to someone?"

She bit her lip, and a pretty pink lip it was.

Alex gave his head a quick shake. He was not here to admire a woman's lips, especially not this woman's. Not someone who did not respect fences and boundaries but interfered with his well-ordered life.

Marley peeked up. "She was my biological father's foster mom for a couple of years."

He took a step back, slamming his calf against the wooden step. Wow, those words had been packed with a lot of anguish. Drama he knew little about, thank the Lord, coming from middle-class parentage. He was fourth of five siblings and had been raised in a solid Christian home with his Italian nonna and most of his uncles, aunts, and cousins living within a few blocks. He'd had it good. He knew that.

But it wasn't reason enough to let his neighbor run roughshod over him or make a play for his sympathy. "Get your chickens out of here and patch the hole in the fence." Had that been too rude? "Please," he added.

Her spine straightened and her eyes skewered his. "There's no hole."

Alex raised his eyebrows. "So how did they get into my yard, then? They're your birds, and it's your duty to keep them contained."

From beside him, Eden spoke in a wry tone. "And it's my duty to make sure the property is left with no more than five birds. So, if you'll round up that one, please, I'll put her in the kennel, and we'll go count what's remaining next door."

Marley's eyes filled with tears. "But you can't."

"Honey." Eden's voice sounded like Marley had gotten on her last nerve. "City regulations are clear. You have too many chickens, and I'm removing some of them. It's my job."

"What will happen to them?" Marley's lips quivered.

Lips again. Alex jerked his gaze away. Either his new neighbor was the ultimate drama queen or she truly felt deeply for those stupid birds. Could she really be this good an actor?

"Hopefully we can find a good home for them." Eden sighed. "Would you please grab that hen?"

"You said you had chickens of your own. Surely you

understand." Marley's gaze brightened. "Maybe you could take them yourself."

"My lot is the same size as yours, and I'm maxed out with a goat and two hens."

Those blue eyes widened. "You have a goat?" she asked in breathless wonder.

She couldn't possibly be performing. "Eden's goat's name is Pansy," offered Alex. "Good milk."

"You know each other." It wasn't a question.

"Bridgeview is a tight neighborhood. Everyone knows everyone." And Alex liked it that way. It was uncomfortable for people who had things to hide, though Alex's brother Basil had managed to mask a drinking problem before running a police roadblock nearly two years back and getting slapped with a DUI. After his jail time, he'd moved to Seattle, claiming Spokane was too claustrophobic. Other than that Basil had left Bridgeview Backyards in the lurch, Alex was glad to see his brother gone.

"Please help me find a home for them," Marley pleaded. She turned to Alex. "Maybe you? I can take care of them here. You don't need to worry about a thing."

His jaw dropped. "Are you kidding me? Have you seen the mess they made? We're running an organic food box program. I'm not giving you an easy out."

She swallowed hard and looked down. "I understand."

Everything she thought flew across her face. He hated being manipulated, but, man! How could he say no to her? Yet, he had to stand firm. His business depended on it.

ABOUT THE AUTHOR

Valerie Comer lives where food meets faith in her real life, her fiction, and on her blog and website. She and her husband of over 35 years farm, garden, and keep bees on a small farm in Western Canada, where they grow and preserve much of their own food.

Valerie has always been interested in real food from scratch, but her conviction has increased dramatically since God blessed her with four delightful granddaughters. In this world of rampant disease and pollution, she is compelled to do what she can to make these little girls' lives the best she can. She helps supply healthy food — local food, organic food, seasonal food — to grow strong bodies and minds.

Valerie is a *USA Today* bestselling author and a two-time Word Award winner. She is known for writing engaging characters, strong communities, and deep faith laced with humor into her green clean romances.

To find out more, visit her website www.valeriecomer.com where you can read her blog, and explore her many links. You can also find Valerie blogging with other authors of Christian contemporary romance at Inspy Romance.

Why not join her email list where you will find news, giveaways, deals, book recommendations, and more? Your thank-you gift is *Promise of Peppermint*, the prequel novella to the Urban Farm Fresh Romance series.

http://valeriecomer.com/subscribe

CPSIA information can be obtained
at www.ICGtesting.com
Printed in the USA
BVHW031100150820
586517BV00001B/115

9 781988 068497